Wesleyan Met

Wesleyan Juvenile Offering. A Miscellany of Missionary Information for young persons

Vol. 21: for the year 1864

SALZWASSER VERLAG

Wesleyan Methodist Missionary Society

Wesleyan Juvenile Offering. A Miscellany of Missionary Information for young persons

Vol. 21: for the year 1864

Reprint of the original, first published in 1864.

1st Edition 2022 | ISBN: 978-3-75259-358-7

Verlag (Publisher): Salzwasser Verlag GmbH, Zeilweg 44, 60439 Frankfurt, Deutschland
Vertretungsberechtigt (Authorized to represent): E. Roepke, Zeilweg 44, 60439 Frankfurt, Deutschland
Druck (Print): Books on Demand GmbH, In de Tarpen 42, 22848 Norderstedt, Deutschland

WESLEYAN JUVENILE OFFERING:

A Miscellany

OF

MISSIONARY INFORMATION

FOR YOUNG PERSONS.

VOL. XXI.

FOR THE YEAR 1864.

LONDON

1864.

CONTENTS OF THE TWENTY-FIRST VOLUME.

LIST OF EMBELLISHMENTS.

A TODA VILLAGE IN THE NEILGHERRY HILLS.

THE

WESLEYAN JUVENILE OFFERING.

CONVERSATION BETWEEN MAMMA AND HER LITTLE GIRL

RESPECTING THE "TODAS," THE OLDEST TRIBE INHABITING THE NEILGHERRIES (BLUE MOUNTAINS).

Kathy.—Mamma, what kind of people are those who came selling honeycomb this morning? They are not like any I ever saw anywhere but here.

Mamma—They are "Todas" or "Toddavaroo." The man and woman that you saw came from a "mund" or village, which we took sister Emily to see last year.

K.—O mamma, will you take me? I should like to see their houses, which Emily said were such strange places.

M.—The walk, my dear, would be too long for you, and you would not be able to cross the ravine, nor climb the rocks which lie in the way. The munds are in very secluded places, which the people select chiefly on account of grass for their buffaloes, the only animals they keep. If you will bring my writing-case, I will show you a sketch which Uncle H. made for the "Juvenile Offering," and which will give you a very correct idea of a Toda mund.

K.—What strange little houses, mamma! they look like large barrels cut in halves along the sides, and set on the ground. How do the people go in and out?

M.—They have to creep in and out through the little door which you see at the end, which is not more than thirty inches in height and twenty-four inches in breadth. The houses themselves are not very large for a family to live in: they are not more than twelve feet long and eight feet broad; and at the highest part, just in the middle, are about seven feet high. The roof is of thatch, very neatly put on, and supported by a half-circular frame-work. Along the sides and at the ends are placed thick, rough planks of wood. There are no windows or chimneys, so that the poor people must find it very dark and smoky.

K.—I am glad, mamma, that I do not live in such a house. Did you go in and see the inside?

M.—No, my dear, but Uncle H. once did. I suppose he must have crept in like a Toda. I stooped down, and looked into one of the houses. On one side a few stones were placed on the ground for a fire-place; on the other side was a raised place built of mud, on which lay a girl, rolled up in a cloth, sleeping; wood was piled up at the further end; and a few chatties, some of brass and some of clay, with two or three bamboo measures, seemed to be all their household furniture.

K.—Mamma, I see only five houses: what a small village it must be.

M.—Yes, seldom more than three or four families reside in one village. The three houses near each other are the dwellings; the one unlike the others in shape is a shed for the buffaloes; and the one in the distance, on the right hand, is the sacred house, into which only the priest is allowed to enter.

K.—What idol do they worship, mamma?

M.—They say they do not worship any idol; and when papa once looked into one of their sacred houses he could not see any thing like an idol. As far as we can learn from them, some kind of worship is offered to the milk which is taken from the buffaloes. It is the duty of the priest to milk the buffaloes: no one else is allowed to do this, and the milk is at once taken into the sacred house. A youth of about fourteen years of age is generally set apart as the priest, but if he gets married another is appointed in his place. The Todas are not known to offer any sacrifice, except in connection with the death of some of their people, when a buffalo or buffaloes are sacrificed; and the flesh is taken away and eaten by another tribe of the inhabitants of the hills. It seems as if they thought the slain buffaloes would accompany their departed friends into another world.

K.—Have they no rice or rajee-fields, mamma? I do not see any in the picture.

M.—No, my dear; neither rice nor rajee grows on these hills; but these Todas do not cultivate the ground for any purpose, or sow any kind of seed: they seem to regard themselves as lords of the soil, and expect the "Burghers" (or Bardagaroo) to bring them, as tribute, a portion of all the grain which they grow; and this is generally done, although of course the land belongs to our Government. The Todas never eat animal food, so that with the milk from their buffaloes, the tribute of grain from the Bardagaroo, and the little things from the bazaar, which they get in exchange for "ghee" (butter), their wants are supplied. Beside, they do not usually stay long enough in the same place at one time to allow of their sowing and reaping.

K.—Why, mamma?

M.—You will think their habits as strange as their houses. Like our own forefathers, many hundreds of years ago, they lead a wandering life. Seeking pasturage for their buffaloes, they occupy the most fertile little slopes, in retired places; and when the grass is all eaten in one place, they move on to another. Thus, like the ancient Britons, they do not settle down in one place.

K.—O mamma! surely the Britons were never like the Todas!

M.—In some respects they were even worse. They roved about from place to place, lived in rude huts, clothed themselves with the skins of animals, and stained their bodies with the juice of a sea-weed. But, worse than this, they offered their children in sacrifice to idols. This the Todas are not guilty of. It is only the blessed Gospel of our Saviour Jesus Christ, which papa and others have come hither to make known, that has made us to differ from the heathen of this and other lands.

(*To be continued.*)

NEWS ABOUT HUDSON'S BAY.

I DARE say most of my young readers have heard or read of Hudson's Bay, and the Indians who live in that cold country. I have got some rather bad news to tell you about them. These Indians are most of them very poor: the way they get a living is to hunt the bear and beaver, and other animals, to get their furs, and sell them, that they may buy food and other necessaries. Sometimes when these men are hunting they get killed, and then their poor wives and children are badly off indeed, for the women cannot go hunting. There are Missionaries living among these Indians, and they and the Missionaries' wives are very kind to the poor Indians: they not only care for their souls, and tell them about Christ and heaven, but they care for the bodies of these poor Indians. The Missionaries' wives have written to their friends in England, from time to time, to ask them to send out some warm clothing for the Indian women and children.

It is only once a year that any thing can go to Hudson's Bay. One ship is sent by the Hudson's-Bay Company to carry the things that are wanted; and last summer, when the ship left, she had on board several cases of nice warm clothes for the Missionaries to give to the Indians: there were some for Norway House, some for Oxford House, some for Mr. Woollsey, the Missionary near the Rocky Mountains.

The ship left in June, and should have arrived in port about the end of August; but, alas! a letter came the other day to say that the ship had met with very bad weather, and could not get to Hudson's Bay, but had been driven into Newfoundland. If you look into the map you will see that the ship has to go a long way round to the north, where the Esquimaux live, before they can get into Hudson's Bay. There are large icebergs in these seas, and I dare say the ship met with some of these icebergs, and was not able to get on.

Now very likely it does not seem such a very great misfortune to you that the ship did not get in when she was expected; but it is a real distress to the Indians, because now they will have to wait a whole year before they get their clothing. The icebergs will be getting larger and larger, and the sea will freeze all round the coast, and no ship can get into the bay, and the poor shivering Indians will have to do without the nice warm garments that the kind friends in England have sent them.

We will walk
in the name of the
Lord our God
for ever and ever.

MICAH iv. 5.

DETERMINED I am, through Jesus' grace,
To walk in his name, to walk in his ways;
With constant endeavour to practise his word,
And own Him for ever, my God and my Lord.

LAPLAND WOMAN AND CHILD.

THERE is one people in Europe who wander about from place to place, yet always keep among the mountains of Norway, on the plains on the north of

Sweden. These people are called Lapps. They have no land, but instead of land they have reindeer. They wander about that they may find pasture for their deer.

The Lapps have nothing to eat but their reindeer,

except a little bread they get from Sweden, because corn will not grow in their country. They have a great abundance of milk from their deer, and it is a great comfort to them, for it is very rich and sweet.

Some of the Lapps reside in towns. The wandering tribes dwell in conical huts supported upon poles, covered with a kind of coarse cloth: around the inside they suspend their few household implements and articles of food. The women dress in dark woollen garments; the men in leather coats and trowsers, with skin-boots. Their infants are nursed in cradles, similar to those used by the North-American Indians, suspended from a pole across the huts. Our picture represents a Lapp mother swinging her little treasure to sleep, packed and strapped in the cradle.

How useful the reindeer are to the Lapps! they could not live without them: no wonder their masters are so fond of them. But he has also two faithful dogs, who help him to manage his reindeer. These clever little dogs are not afraid when the wolves come. The timid deer run up and down the mountains, not knowing how to get away from the howling wolves: then the dogs drive them all together, and, standing round them, keep off their enemies; therefore, when the Lapp returns home tired in the evening, he shares his soup and his meat with his brave guards.

(To be continued.)

JESUS shall have dominion
  O'er river, sea, and shore,—
Far as the eagle's pinion,
  Or dove's light wing can soar.

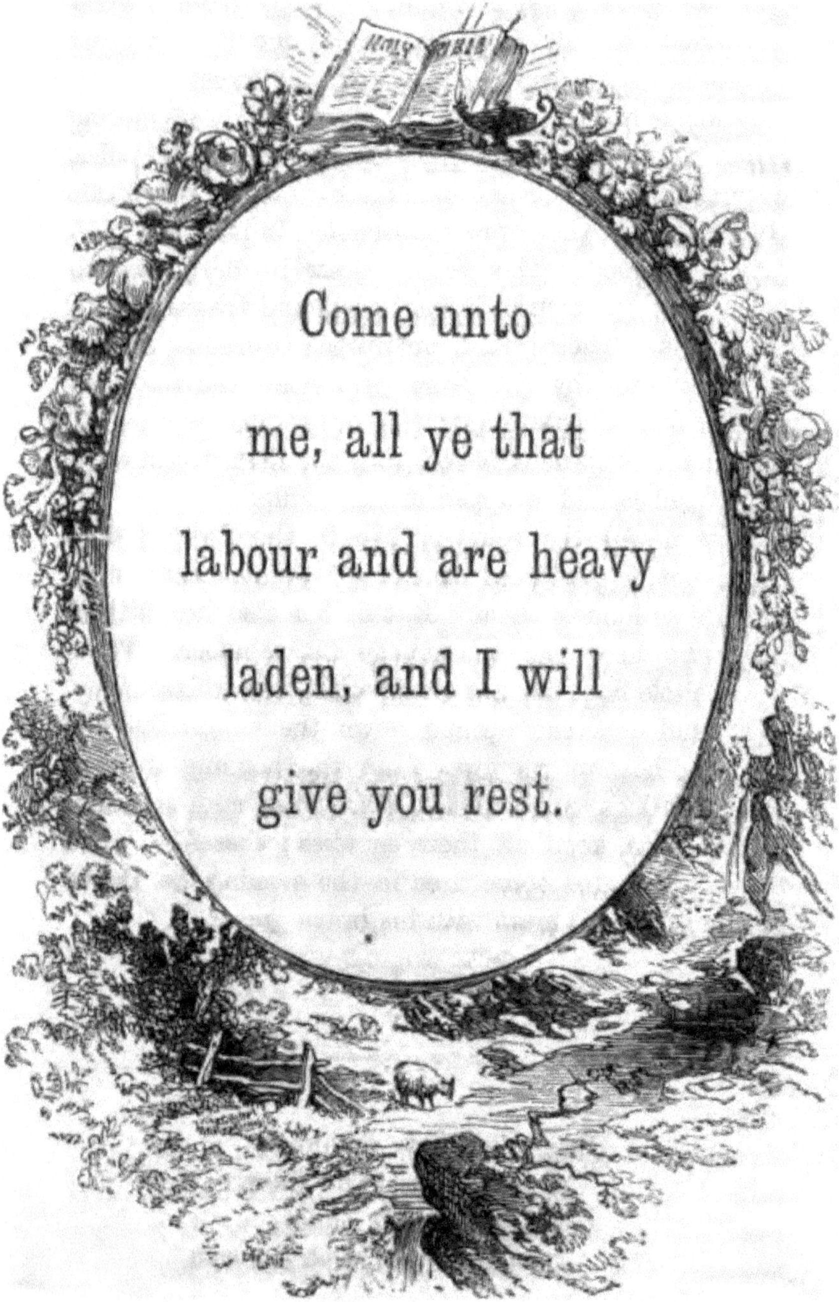

Come unto
me, all ye that
labour and are heavy
laden, and I will
give you rest.

A BABY IDOL.

In heathen countries the idols are generally of stone, or brass, or wood, but there is a country in Asia called Thibet, where they have a LIVING IDOL. It is a man, and he is called the GRAND LAMA. He is looked up to as the greatest being in the world by all the people in that large country.

When one Lama dies, another is chosen,—some little baby,—and he is placed in a very grand palace, and worshipped as a god all his life long.

I have heard of one of these baby Lamas, who, when only eighteen months old, sat up with great majesty on his pile of cushions. When strangers entered, he looked at them kindly, and when they made a speech to him, he bowed his little head very graciously.

What a sad fate for this poor infant! To be set up as a god, and taught to think himself a god, while all the time he is a helpless, foolish, dying, sinful creature.

FAR OFF.

A STORY FROM FIJI.

"Verily there is a God that judgeth in the earth."

I HAVE just received a letter from Mr. Horsley, who is a Missionary in Fiji, and in it he tells me the following story:—

"We have just built a beautiful chapel: it was quite finished, and only waiting to be opened. A heathen man, a Fijian, desecrated this house of God by pulling to pieces all the ornamental sinnet work that the people had taken such pains to complete. The beautiful large white shells that adorned the door-posts, communion-rails, and pulpit, were taken away by him to his canoe.

"He then went and sat on his canoe, boasting to those around him of what he had done, when suddenly a spark from his cigar fell into his powder pouch, and in an instant he was blown up. He lingered in much misery for several hours, and then died.

"I overheard a conversation among the chiefs the following morning, when the King said, 'It is a very little matter to fight against us, but when they fight against God in that way, it is most awful.' Both the heathen and the Christians acknowledge the hand of God in this matter."

JUBILEE HYMN.

For fifty years of wonders,
  For soul-redeeming days,
Give thanks as loud as thunders,
  But sweet as angels' praise!
Before our King anointed
  The silver trumpets sound,
And messengers appointed,
  Send all the earth around.

The day of great Atonement,
  The High Priest pleads to-day;
Proclaim the Lamb's enthronement,
  His universal sway;
For while the Priest is pleading,
  The King proclaims his grace,
The spotless Lamb is bleeding,
  And mercy meets our race.

The King the word hath spoken—
  The captives shall be free,
The yokes shall all be broken,
  The world have Jubilee.
The fields the father squandered
  The son again shall hold.
The widow lorn that wandered,
  Have oliveyard and fold.

To Dan's remotest mountain,
  To lone Beersheba's well,
To every desert fountain,
  Where scattered exiles dwell,
Go track the lone one straying,
  Leave not an ear unblest,
The great High Priest is praying,
  And souls shall find their rest.

The Fifty Years before us
  Shall greater wonders see;
Let silver trumps in chorus
  Sound out a Jubilee.
The day of great Atonement,
  The High Priest pleads to-day;
Proclaim the Lamb's enthronement,
  His universal sway.

REV. W. ARTHUR, A.M.

"Then shalt thou cause the trumpet of the jubilee to sound on the tenth day of the seventh month, in the day of atonement shall ye make the trumpet sound throughout all your land."—Lev. xxv. 9.

STORY OF AMON.

TRANSLATED FROM THE FRENCH.

Now I am going to tell you of a little boy whose joy was very great when he had a Bible of his own—the book of God.

His name was Amon. He was four years old when he lost his parents. He went to live with his grandparents, very pious old people, who made him read in the large, old, well-worn Bible, about the love which God has shown us in sending His Son to save sinners.

His grandfather died suddenly, and Amon was very much affected. He and his grandmother found themselves much alone; and both went to seek consolation in the old grandfather's Bible. The boy opened at the resurrection of Lazarus. The poor grandmother wept much, covering her face with her apron; but when she heard these words, "Thy brother shall rise again," she seemed comforted. Amon did not yet comprehend all he read. Afterwards he understood that his grandmother rejoiced that she should see one day those whom she had lost, since those who love God will rise again to be clad with a body immortal and glorious.

At ten years old he fóllowed a shepherd, and took his flocks to pasture. He had learned to knit; and he made stockings while guarding his sheep, which gave him fifteen or twenty centimes a day. Nothing was wanting to make him completely happy but a Bible; but how could he get money enough to buy one?

He went to the Sabbath school. The teacher was a pious man, who spoke constantly of the kindness we ought to feel for each other, and the love we owe the Lord Jesus Christ, who has Himself loved us so much. Amon confided to him his desire to buy a Bible, and confessed that he earned so little that he could not hope to have one for a long time. The teacher advised him to rise earlier and retire later, so he could do more work. He told him also of a place where he could find water-cresses, and said that if he would bring them early on market-days, he was sure the farmers' daughters would buy them to carry with their butter to the city. He added, that he would keep his money as Amon earned it, and promised, when he had a sum sufficient to purchase a Bible, he would take him to a bookseller to choose one. His grandmother, too, who was pleased with Amon, gave him from time to time five centimes, which increased his little treasure.

This poor woman fell sick, and kept her bed several weeks. She could earn nothing during this time; but as soon as her rent was due, the landlord, who was a hard man, sent to demand the amount due to him, and gave only till the evening to procure money. When her little grandson came home, she told him what had passed. "If I cannot pay the six francs which I owe," said she, "they will seize our bed, our torn covering, and this wheel which helps us to live." Hardly had she spoken these words, when Amon rushed out, crying, "I have them! I have them!" He went to his teacher, and said: "Sir, I need my money which you have. You will be very much astonished when you know it is not to buy the Bible. It is to help my grandmother, whom they are about to drive out of her house if she cannot pay her rent. Is it not better to do what the Word of God teaches than to have a Bible of my own?"

The old man was moved to tears in listening. He laid his hand on the boy's head, and said: "May God bless you, and may your old age be full of glory and happiness!"

Amon quickly carried his money to his grandmother,

who received it with joy when the teacher assured her it was honestly earned.

Toward the end of autumn, a young lady in deep mourning came to settle in the village. She had lost her husband, who had been killed in battle. One day, as she walked near the place where Amon pastured his flock, she said to her companion: "Here surely is a child who does not know sorrow."

"Oh yes, madam, I have known it," replied the little boy. "I have lost my grandfather, whom I loved with all my heart; my grandmother is very sick; and I cannot earn money enough to buy a Bible."

"When did your grandfather die?" asked the lady.

"A few months ago; but that is not the greatest of misfortunes, since he has gone to God and the Saviour; and the Bible teaches me I shall go to join him some day."

The young lady went away, looking very kindly upon Amon; and in the evening, when she had learned where his grandmother lived, she sent to her money, medicine, and provisions. Judge, my dear children, of the happiness of that poor woman, who thus received all she needed.

The young widow came to the Sabbath school. She spoke to the teacher, and looked smilingly on his little pupil, who was very happy when he learned that she had given him money; and he fell on his knees to thank God, who had inspired in his benefactress the good thought to give him enough to buy a Bible of his own. Then, after having gone to her house to express his gratitude, he went quickly to purchase his precious book.

THE

WESLEYAN JUVENILE OFFERING.

NEGRO WOMEN IN THE WEST INDIES.

A Missionary's wife was one day taking a class of negro women, who came together to be taught the truths of religion. Instead of talking to them herself, she asked one of them to tell the others in as plain a manner as she could some of the things she had learned about God's way of saving sinners. She did this partly to find out if the woman remembered what she had been told, and partly because some of them were very ignorant, and perhaps they could understand one who would talk to them in their own style better than they would understand her.

It was a very old woman who was asked to speak, and she very readily complied. If you had seen the old negro women sitting round, all stretching out their long necks, and listening to the speaker as though their very life depended upon her words, you could never have forgotten it.

She began—"Well, granny, you must open your ears, and listen good, and I'll tell you ebery ting I 'member about Jesus Christ's story.

"Long time since, before anybody live in Africa, God made dis world. He made all de trees, all de beasts, ebery ting, and when He make 'em done, den He make man. Well, He look. He see de man no have matty; den He make him sleep, so He take piece from de man's side, and make woman. Den He tell de man, 'Look, your wife dere; mind her good.' Den God say to 'em, 'See gauva dere, mango dere, banana dere, plantain dere, ebery ting so good; you may eat 'em, except the one mamy apple in de middle of de garden; you must'nt touch dat; if you do, you shall dead.' So dey two live so good together, till one day de woman was alone. She walk in de garden, she see one big snake on a tree; de snake begin to peak wid de woman; he ask her why she did'nt take de mamy apple off de tree in de middle of de garden. She say, 'Oh, God tell an me not to touch de tree; for if me do, me sa dead.' He say, 'No, you sa not dead; go take it; da tree more better than any of de trees, and God know very well de tree shall do you good. So de woman took some of dem mamy apples; she eat some, and carried some to de man; he too eat 'em. Well, afterward God come down. He call de man; but de man no give answer, for dey both get frighted when dey hear God call 'em. God know dey been touching de tree; so He say to Adam, 'What make you take de mamy apple, after I told you you must'nt touch it?' Den de man put all de blame on de woman. God ax de woman, 'What business you had to touch de tree, after I tell you not?' Den de woman put all de blame on de snake. Well, God was very angry, and He curse de snake; He curse de woman, wid de man, and de ground; He drive 'em out of de garden, and make His angels stand with big cutlass to keep 'em out. Oh, dey two very sorry for taking de fruit. Well, dey look all about, dey see noting. Gauva no dere, mango no dere, banana no dere, plantain no dere; noting at all no dere, but black sage and sour grass.

"Well, God hab one Son up at top. He see all dis trouble, and He know very well dat when His Fader make de bargain wid Adam, it no for he alone, but for all dem pickaninny what shall come. So He peak wid de Fader, and tell Him He sorry for dem people soul; Heself will go and suffer all de punishment for dem. God say, 'Yes, by and by; but dey must try to obey me, and kill plenty of sheep, wid goat and oxen.' So dem people do. Some try best, and some good like Abel; but plenty do bad. Den Jesus Christ did come into dis sinful wicked world. Dey treat Him bad; dey want to kill Him, even while He was a baby. When He grow, He behave so good. Some people go to Him wid blind eye; He make 'em see. Some have lame foot; He make 'em well. Some dead a'ready; He make 'em get out of de coffin. Still dem people no believe: dey say, 'No, it is not Jesus; He one man like an we.' So dey get de policeman to catch Him, carry Him to magistrate, tell lie upon Him, till dey say, 'He must die.' Dey got a tree, and nail piece of wood upon it for his two arms; den dey nailed Jesus to de tree, big nail through his foot, and big nail through his hands: He hang so till He fainty; dey give Him bitter ting to drink; dey strike his side wid sword till He die! All dis He suffer for we poor sinner. What we must do for Jesus for all this?"

Here the tears rolled down the cheeks of the poor women, and the exclamations, "O my beloved Lord!" "Ah, my sweet Saviour!" were heard amidst their sighs and tears.

My children, could you give a better account of the sin of Adam, and the way of salvation through the Lord Jesus, than the negro woman gave? No; the negro woman is before you—before you far; for I fear there are some who have never asked, as she did, "What we must do for Jesus for all this?"

PERILS AMONG THE HEATHEN.

WOULD you like to hear a story that Mr. Champness told me of the peril he was in when he was at Abbeokuta? how he was nearly taken by the fighting women soldiers of the King of Dahomey.

You have heard of these fighting women. The King has an army of them. The business in which they are chiefly employed is seizing slaves, that the King may sell them, and get large sums of money. Very fierce and cruel these women are. They fight as savagely as the men, indeed they are more cruel and fierce than the men; and they are very clever in catching people.

I will tell you how they entrap them. Two hundred perhaps, of these women will go to a place where they think their enemies are likely to pass, and will lie down in the high grass, a hundred on each side of the road. Their dress is a dusky-green sort of colour, so that they are not seen; and travellers, not knowing

ABBEOKUTA.

that the enemy is near, pass along the road. They let them pass for some little way, then rise up, rush on them, and chop them down. There is no running away or chance of escape. When Mr. Champness was in Abbeokuta, the King of Dahomey sent some of thes women soldiers to fight against the Egbas, as the people of Abbeokuta are called. Mr. Champness had heard that they were in the neighbourhood, and thought he would ride out and try if he could see where they were. The road he took was just where these women were lying down on each side of it, and he was riding straight into the trap. A little way before him six men were travelling on the same road. These men were taken, and never seen again. Mr. Champness would soon have shared the same fate; but his friends, hearing which way he had gone, ran after him, and forced him to go back. God was taking care of his servant, and his life was spared.

These women soldiers are dreadfully fierce. A man once took one of them prisoner, and took her home, intending to make her his slave. When he got her in his house, he took off the cords which bound her. As soon as she was free, she seized a loaded gun that was in the corner, and shot the man dead that had taken her. Then the people about her chopped her to pieces.

But why are these people so cruel and wicked? How can you expect them to be otherwise? They have never been taught better: nobody has been to them to tell them of the Gospel of Christ, which teaches men to love one another. There are hundreds of towns in Africa, and tens of thousands of people, who have never heard of Jesus. Hundreds of these Africans are dying every day; and when they appear before the judgment-seat, they will say, "It is eighteen hundred years since Christ came into the world to save sinners, and no one has been to tell us of Him." Oh! my dear children, do let us pray constantly, and pray fervently, that God may put it into the hearts of many men to go to these poor ignorant fellow-creatures. They would be glad to receive the message of salvation; they want to be religious; they want something to worship. One day, as Mr. Champness was travelling, he saw by the road-side two old men with grey hair, kneeling down before an ugly idol, and praying to it; and they were praying devoutly and earnestly, as men pray when they want to be saved from evil. If these poor old grey-headed men had known of Christ, how gladly would they have gone to Him! but they knew Him not: they had nothing better than an ugly idol to worship.

"Shepherd of souls, with pitying eye,
The thousands of the heathen see;
To thee in their behalf we cry,
Ourselves but newly found in thee.

"See where o'er desert wastes they err,
And neither food nor feeder have,
Nor fold, nor place of refuge near;
For no man cares their souls to save."

A NIGHT IN THE WILDERNESS.

A MISSIONARY TRAVELLING IN SOUTH AFRICA.

A LONG and toilsome day's ride to the water. During the succeeding night we had no sleep. We had to watch all night armed, and with large fires to keep the ravenous beasts from our oxen and horses. Many a howling I had formerly heard in the wilderness; but such an awful concert I never experienced before. An incredible number of hyænas had taken up their quarters near the water, and devoured, with the demon-like yells, the poor animals that stole to the water to quench their thirst in the dark of night. They repeatedly made a thrust at our waggons; but, thank God, we sustained no injury. At times it seemed as if the evil spirits had a forepost in this locality. Jackals, wild dogs, lions, all supported the chorus, so that we were heartily glad when the sun came forth.

SABBATH SCHOOL IN RUSSIA.

You have seen several pictures of schools in foreign lands, but we have never shown you a Russian school. Here we have a representation of a Sabbath school in Russia. And is it not a group of *earnest* faces? The teachers are earnest and the scholars are earnest, and nearly all are giving their fixed attention. Ah! such is the attention that always makes interested and earnest teachers.

The Missionaries connected with the German Mission have extended their labours into Russia, and many have become true Christians. But the converts are subject to severe persecution. Still the word of God advances.

How thankful we should be that the Sabbath school, with all its attractions and blessings, is extending to other lands, so that we can say—

"Lord of the Sabbath, hear thy praise,
In other lands, which children raise;
Who meet together on thy day,
To read and learn, to sing and pray!"

CONVERSATION BETWEEN MAMMA AND HER LITTLE GIRL

RESPECTING THE "TODAS," THE OLDEST TRIBE INHABITING THE NEILGHERRIES (BLUE MOUNTAINS).

(*Continued.*)

K.—What language do the Todas speak, mamma? Can papa talk with them?

M.—Their own language is very strange, made up almost entirely of very little words, most of them having a harsh sound; but they understand Canarese, and when papa spoke to them about God and the Saviour, they seemed attentive; but as soon as he had done, they were clamorous for "illam, illam," (a present). This they seem to expect from every European. Once when I said that I had brought no money, one of the women said, "Why, then, did you come here?"

K.—Why do the Bardagaroo give grain and other things to the Todas? were these hills theirs at first?

M.—The Todas are the earliest known inhabitants of the Neilgherries; but we cannot trace their early history. Their own notion seems to be that their forefathers were created on these hills. For a long time they were the only inhabitants; then came up from the plains a few "Cotars," who were allowed to cultivate portions of land, on the condition that they gave a certain portion to the Todas as tribute. Soon after this, perhaps about three or four hundred years ago, some Bardagaroo came up from the plains, probably from the north-east, and were allowed to cultivate land on the same terms as the Cotars. There are now several thousands of these Bardagaroo on the hills, but the Todas still require the tribute.

K.—Yes, mamma, I see a great many more Bardages than I do Todas, and it is very easy to know one from the other, for the Todas do not wear turbans on their heads, and, beside, they are a much finer looking people.

M.—It is said that there are not more than six hundred Todas all over the hills. They are certainly a very fine race, not like any other Hindoos that we see. Tall and well formed, with fine eyes, a roman nose, and generally a good expression of countenance: they are easily distinguished. You observe that they do not wear turbans: their hair, about which they seem rather particular, forms a good covering for the head. It is cut about six inches long all round, and generally parted in the middle from the crown. Most of the women have fine long black ringlets, which hang loosely on their necks.

K.—But, mamma, don't you think they look dirty?

M.—Yes; I fancy they seldom wash the one cloth which forms their whole dress. The one cloth is about five yards in length, and about two yards in breadth, and is thrown about the person in a very careless way. The men wear it down to the knee, but the women allow it to descend to the ancle. The women are very fond of ornaments on their neck and arms, but they are of little value, being chiefly made of brass or shells.

K.—What books do they read, mamma?

M.—They seem to have nothing like books among them; and papa says he has met with only one among them who knew even any letters: this was a boy who had learned to read a little in a school belonging to the German Mission. They are very ignorant and very idle; but they are included among those for whom the Gospel is intended, and we hope they will be instructed, and brought to know that blessed Saviour who hath died for them, and is able to save them. We must pray for them. I have now told you most of what is known about this singular race.

K.—Thank you, mamma; I will not forget the Todas when we go down from the hills, and I should be very glad to hear that they could read the Bible, and that they had become Christians.

Ootacamund, August 1863.

OUR REFUGE.

UPON life's stormy sea
  We all in peril ride;
But God hath given His Son to be
  An Ark upon the tide.

We love the tale to tell
  To heathen lands afar,
Till all who now in darkness dwell
  Hail Christ, the Morning Star.

But when the waves rose high,
  And clouds spread thick and dark,
And Noah and his family
  Entered the sheltering ark,

Did each, whose busy hand
  Had helped that ark to build,
Within its refuge safely stand,
  When rose the tempest wild?

Dear Lord! with anxious care,
  Help *us* to look within,
And see what idol reigneth there,
  What dearly cherished sin.

All must before Thee stand;
  How shall *we* meet Thine eye,
If, children of a Christian land,
  Without the Ark we die?

A STORY ABOUT LAPLAND.

For a long, long while the Laplanders were heathens; and though they now call themselves Christians, they are very ignorant, for they have been taught very little.

There are, however, Missionaries among them. One of them is a Swede, and his name is Tellstrom. He was a poor man in Stockholm, working hard in painting houses, when it came into his heart to go to Lapland. But he did not know the Lappish language, nor did he know any one who could teach him. However, he had heard that a Lappish grammar had been printed. He inquired for it in all the booksellers' shops, but could not meet with it. At last he obtained leave to search for it amongst a number of old books stored up in a warehouse, and, to his great joy, he found it. In all his spare time (and he had not much) he studied it; and he made great progress, for he looked to God for help. He soon got a Lappish Testament, and learned to read it.

But *how* was he to go to Lapland? He knew a good gentleman in Stockholm, a Missionary, named Mr. Scott. He went to him and told him his plan. Mr. Scott was surprised, for only a short time before he had received some money from England, with this message, "Spend the money in doing good to the poor Lapps." "Now," thought Mr. Scott, "this is wonderful: the money comes first, and then the man who wants to do good to these Lapps: surely God sends both the money and the man.

Mr. Scott consulted with his friends respecting the painter, and they all talked to Tellstrom about it.

They asked him, "Have you learned that difficult language?"

"Yes," he said; and he told them how he had found the grammar.

"Can you bear the cold?" said they.

"Yes," he replied; and he told them how he had tried whether he could bear cold by walking on the stone stairs in winter without shoes or stockings.

"Can you bear hunger, and can you live without bread and vegetables?"

"Yes," he replied. "I have accustomed myself to fast. Every Sabbath I have fasted, because I would not work, and I had not money to buy food without working."

"Can you bear to be without a friend in a country where true Christians are very scarce?"

"Yes, I can bear even that, for Christ has said, 'Lo, I am with you alway, even unto the end of the world.'"

Mr. Scott and his friends agreed that Tellstrom was fit to be a Missionary, but they thought he ought first to gain more knowledge. So they said, "We will give you money to keep you without working, that you may have time for study." Therefore Tellstrom left off painting, and spent his time in reading. Yet he refused to accept any money. How, then, did he live? He had a silver spoon: his godmother, a noble lady, had given it to him when he was baptized: he sold it for food. He had never sold it while he was a painter, though he had often wanted food, because a spoon given by a great person to a poor one at his baptism is considered a treasure; but now he sold it for the work of God.

At last the time came for Tellstrom to go to Lapland. A Missionary Society was formed. There are many in England, but this was the first in Sweden; and Tellstrom was the first Missionary sent out. He went to Lapland in the year 1835. Just before he went, a friend gave him a silver spoon—a friend who knew nothing of his having sold a spoon. Tellstrom was surprised. He thought he saw in this little gift a sign that the Lord would give him back *all* he had given up for his sake, and therefore he had these words of Christ engraved upon the new spoon—"There is no man that hath left house, or parents, or brethren, or wife, or children, for the kingdom of God's sake, who shall not receive manifold more in this present time, and in the world to come, life everlasting."

Upon Tellstrom's arrival in Lapland he hired a room, and preached at first in the Swedish tongue; and God was with him, and the people heard him gladly, and so filled the room, that he began to preach in the church. But he did not long preach there, for the Lapps are a wandering people, because their deer are wandering creatures, seeking moss where they can find it. Therefore Tellstrom became a wanderer too, that he might gain the more souls. He learned, in summer, to pick his way through the marshes on the roads made of pine trees, that shake under the traveller's tread; and he ventured in winter to cross the frozen plains where no foot of man is to be seen; and once he nearly lost his life amidst the snowy deserts.

He longed to instruct the little ones, and took eighteen of them under his care, and fed, and clothed, and taught them for two years; then sent them home with little books in their hands, and sweet hymns on their lips, to cheer their parents' huts with prayers and praises.

Then he received another company of children into his house, and in two years he sent them forth to make room for yet another little band. In this manner he taught a great number of children; and many parents, through the children, have turned unto the Lord.

How pleasant it would be to visit one of the huts where these pious families live, and to hear them thanking God for sending his servant to tell them of Jesus! NEAR HOME.

A STORY ABOUT MISS CAMERON'S OBEDIENT LITTLE SCHOOL-CHILDREN.

MISS CAMERON has a school in Natal, South Africa. Her scholars are very fond of her, because she is so kind to them, and teaches them so nicely. They are very lively children, and must be always doing something; and often it is rather hard work to keep them properly employed. They are very fond of their school, and often get there before their governess. Then they watch for her coming; and as soon as they catch sight of her, they run to meet and welcome her.

The climate of Natal is generally very pleasant; but sometimes they have very heavy rain, such rain as we do not see in this country, excepting now and then, when we have a heavy thunder-storm. When it rains so heavily Miss Cameron does not know how to get to the school: there are no cabs or omnibusses that she can go in: she must walk. So it happens sometimes that she has to wait for the rain to moderate before she can go to the school. The children are carried to the school, and are there before her. They cannot run out to meet her in the rain, so they keep in the school. One morning, when Miss Cameron was detained by the weather, on arriving at the school she found the children were making much noise. She was not pleased, and she told the little girls that *good children* minded what their teacher told them as much when she was absent as when she was present, and that they should be quiet when they got to school, and not make a noise when she was not there. The next rainy day, when Miss Cameron was late, she was surprised, as she got near to the school, to hear no noise; every thing was quiet. On going in, she found the children all seated in their places, very quiet and good, and some of the bigger girls acting as monitors, and keeping order. Don't you think she was much pleased to find the children were so good and obedient?

THE

WESLEYAN JUVENILE OFFERING.

To my Young Friends,

The sun had just risen on a beautiful October morning in India, when we started on our way to visit a sacred place, called Nunjingode. The dew-drops were yet sparkling on the leaves, and a gentle breeze made the air cool and refreshing; for my little friends must remember that an October morning in India is very different from one at home.

Now we were passing a field of the castor-oil plant; then a garden of plantains, which is a delicious fruit, something like a fine juicy pear, though of a very different shape; then a number of palm-trees, such as you see in pictures of India, would attract our attention. About half way we met a group of pilgrims. These are persons who have come a very long way to some holy place, because they think, if they do so, the god who lives there will be pleased, and will give them what they want. Well, these poor people looked so weary, for they had been walking for many days, you would have felt quite sorry to see them. A little further on we met others, all going to visit Nunjingode, which they think is a very sacred place. A bend of the road now brought us full in view of the river Capila, whose bright waters flow past Nunjingode.

Leaving our conveyance under the shade of a spreading tree, we walked up to see the great temple. On our way, the first thing we noticed made us feel very, very sad. A beautiful young Brahmin lady, richly dressed, was measuring every step from the river to the temple, by throwing herself on the ground, and laying her bright young head in the dust. She was followed by a boy, who did just the same. We were told that she had come from Mysore along with her husband, who was very sick, in hopes that this trouble would please the god and induce it to heal the poor suffering man, who was then lying under a porch of the temple. We watched the young wife performing her weary task, which she did with such earnestness and such sorrow in her large beautiful eye, as made our hearts ache, while her lips moved as if in prayer. Poor thing, well might she submit to toil and pain, if the blow she dreaded might not fall on her; for, as soon as death should take away the husband of her youth, those gold necklaces and ear-rings must be laid off for ever, her fine dark air be closely shaven off, and a life of shame and suffering would immediately begin.

India, my young friends, has no tear of pity for the widow or orphan; but God Almighty counts every sigh that rises from the despised one. We had by this time reached the temple, which is the largest I have yet seen. Its great gateway, its two grand pagodas with their gilded horns flashing in the sunbeams, the crowd of priests and religious beggars with their horns, from which they blew a long wailing blast now and again, made us feel a sort of woe. In the courtyard incense was burning in little vessels, and people were passing out and in with offerings of fruit or honied water, &c., which they pour upon the idol. A tame elephant walked about inside, gathering up the leaves that were strewn round with its trunk.

As we stood looking on sadly, a band of pilgrims came up from the river, their long dishevelled hair hanging round their haggard faces and necks. One of them had, because of a vow, left his hair so long uncombed, that it hung round his body like long dusty ropes. Each held in his devoutly clasped hands a flower, which he meant to present to the idol. On reaching the front of the temple they threw themselves flat on the ground, and rolled in the dust all along to the other side, where a priest raised them up. This they must do three times, when, having bathed in the holy waters of the Capila, they are allowed to enter and see the god. We then sat down in a kind of tent opposite, and saw, not men only, bu' women and little children doing the same, and then gathering up the dust to rub on their foreheads. These things made my heart almost sicken, and I could scarcely bear to look longer. Oh, what would the happy boys and girls of our own dear land have felt, if they had stood there and remembered, as we did, that the great God who gave the first and second commandments was looking down with anger on those poor blinded idolaters?

For nearly two hours did my husband try to shew them their awful danger, and teach them that our God and their God is love; that He has no pleasure in their pain and misery; but that He so loved them as to give His own Son, in order to save them, and that Jesus was waiting to save the very worst one among them without money or price, if they would but come to Him.

As we felt weary, and an Indian sun was blazing overhead, we returned to our "bandy" under the tree. Many followed us to hear more, and to receive books from the Missionary. We remained there about three hours longer, during which time the people burnt a corpse just a little way from us on the bank of the river, this being their common practice.

Will not these things, my dear young friends, lead you to thank God every day that you were never taught to pray to a stone idol, as the boys and girls of India are? Will they not make you love that blessed Saviour who has loved you so much, and lead you to pity and pray for the poor heathen, and those who try to teach them? Trusting you will, I am your sincere friend, J. HUTCHEON.

City of Mysore, India.

All nations
whom thou hast
made shall come
and worship
before thee,
O Lord;
and shall glorify
thy name.

Psalm lxxxvi. 9.

XAVIER, THE MISSIONARY MONK.

MANY years ago there was a time when Christian people thought little or nothing about the poor heathen. When people wished to serve God they thought they could do nothing better than shut themselves up and lead a lonely life of self-denial and prayer. The world was so wicked they did not like to live in it, but they forgot that God wants his people to work in this wicked world, and try to make it better; to teach the ignorant, and set a good example, and do all the good they can.

There was a young man named Francis Xavier, who lived in the north of Italy in those times. He had been very worldly and fond of pleasure, but he had a friend who persuaded him to give up all and devote himself to the service of God. So Xavier became a monk, and he also became a very holy and devoted man, and all his desire was to go to the poor heathen and teach them the name of Jesus. After a few years of hard work, preaching and toiling among the poor at home, he was appointed to go to India. All he took with him was a Bible, a breviary, a silver cup, and a crucifix, for you must remember he was a Roman-Catholic monk. He was more than a year on the voyage, which seems a very long time to us. He had no money, but the captain gave him his passage free, and he spent his time in acts of kindness to the passengers, many of whom were very ill. He arrived first at Goa, a Portuguese settlement in India, where the people professed to be Christians; but Xavier was shocked to find that they were as wicked, if not worse, than the poor heathen around them.

He hardly knew what to do at first, but this was the plan he tried, and you will agree with me that it was a very wise one. He walked about the streets with a bell, and collected all the little children round him, and then he took them into the church, for they had a church, though they had almost forgotten to use it. He could not teach them much at first, but he taught them to say "Our Father" and the Creed, and he told them about the Saviour; and then, when the children went home, they repeated these things to their parents. The parents' hearts were touched at hearing these good words from the little ones' lips, and when Xavier went to see them himself they listened willingly to him as he reminded them that they were Christians, and not heathen, and tried to persuade them to lead better lives. When he had worked hard among them, and preached to them and taught them, he went further into the country, and set to work among the Hindoos. He worked hard for eleven years among them, travelling many thousands of miles, teaching Christianity to thousands of people, and leaving love and a spotless name behind him wherever he went. At last, worn

out with labours, he died on a lonely shore in a strange land, with no earthly comforts, and only one faithful attendant near him, but with his soul at rest, rejoicing and triumphing in God, and with a bright hope of receiving the crown that is laid up for all faithful martyrs and Missionaries of the Gospel, and for all faithful Christian people in all ages of the world.

TOMB IN INDIA.

My dear Children,—You have before you a picture of a Mohammedan mausoleum, or tomb, in Madras, which is built, as you see, like a small mosque, with minarets on the top, and which stands in a garden, with smaller tombs and graves round it.

Now a mausoleum is a magnificent tomb or monument, generally erected by rich people to contain the dead bodies of their greatest and most illustrious relatives, and in this one probably lies the chief of some great family, though who he was, what his name, or what he was famous for, I never heard, though I often passed by this grand tomb of his. There is nothing remarkable about the inside of the place: it contains only one large room, perfectly dark, and without seats, fittings up, or decorations whatever. In the midst of it stands the man's tomb, built of stone, just like the square tombs you see in your own churchyards in England.

On the anniversaries of his death, his friends bring garlands of flowers, and rose-water, and scatter them about the floor, chanting a sort of funeral dirge, in which they praise his goodness, his handsome turban, his valiant deeds, and call out to him by name, something like this—"O son of Mohammed, why didst thou die? Noble, learned man, why didst thou die? Alas! alas! thou who wert in the possession of so many and great riches, why, alas! didst thou die?' The door is always left open, and a Mussulman may at any time enter and offer up his prayers there.

The fashion of erecting mausoleums appears to have been a very early one, for the first we read of was built by Artemisia, Queen of Halicarnassus, as the tomb of her husband Mausolus, B.C. 352. And the last we hear of is that one at Frogmore, where lies the body of our beloved Prince—Albert the Good—also built by a Queen in memory of her husband. Oh, dear children, how many tears, and sighs, and prayers must that place have witnessed! They cannot wake the dead, but they will be heard in heaven by Jesus, who knows how to comfort the afflicted, and who careth for the fatherless and for the widow.

LETTER FROM SAMOA.

A TRUE "TALA" ABOUT A LITTLE ENEMY.

My dear young Friends—You have heard, no doubt, about a number of islands, many thousands of miles away from England, called Samoa. It was till lately a heathen land. They never heard of the Saviour till about thirty-three years ago.

Now, if you please, I will give you a true account of a little enemy they have amongst them. It is called an "*ane*." You never saw such a little enemy as this *ane* is, so that I will tell you how I have seen it.

We were at the tea-table last evening, and, in addition to other things, a kind native had brought us four little fishes called *atule*, which my little boy and girl, and myself, were heartily enjoying to our tea, when down came master *ane* into the plate. Perhaps you think he came to steal our *atule:* no such thing, he isn't big enough for that. Right glad was I to see him in trouble, the little enemy, for I thought, It just serves him right. There he is now, just no bigger than a grain of rice, and with wings too, which, somehow, he can doff and throw away as you would an old bonnet before you got the new one. He is a fearful little enemy, either with or without wings. Nothing scarcely can escape him in Samoa except iron and stone, and living creatures who are a match for him. He digs and bores through books and paper like a digger in a gold mine, until they are like perforated cardboard. He eats up chairs, and tables, and wooden bedsteads, like sweet cake. Housebreaking is a very little thing with this little enemy. Though he can't do it all at once, yet he breaks down strong doors and windows in a very short time. He can't pull down pillars, but he can eat them down. Houses often crumble to dust before him. He is indeed a fearful little enemy. If he peeps into a box it is to destroy it; if he climbs a post it is to destroy it; if he looks through a bookcase it is to destroy it; if he enters a house it is to destroy it; if he goes on board a boat he means to destroy it; if he looks at a dress he intends to eat it; if he goes up stairs he will break them, if they are made of wood; if he finds out the pianoforte he is sure to stop the playing: indeed, he revels in ruin.

Pray what shall we compare master *ane* to? or who is he like? Call him sin, shall we? Sin and Ane both seem little things, and both work very quietly, but both do dreadful things.

A little while ago a large beam fell from the roof of

a Mission house in Samoa, and smashed the corner of a table in the sitting-room because master *ane* was up in the roof. One day a shower of apples fell over the wall of an orchard because master Sin was up in the tree, and the poor boys who helped him were brought into great trouble about the apples. If we compare master *ane* to a steam-engine off the line, then we must call his carriages ruin. *Ane* runs and ruin follows, so Sin runs and ruin follows. But I must not tire you, and shall only add that master *ane's* name in England is white ant.

MARTIN DYSON.

AFRICAN LADIES AT BREAKFAST.

A MISSIONARY who was at St. Mary's, in Western Africa, was invited by a merchant to his home to see how the native ladies took their breakfast. The merchant's lady entertained a company of ladies of her own class, at a breakfast on coos-coos, the most delicate preparation of native corn food used there: it is made of the smallest kind of grain, pounded in a mortar, and in some way mysterious to strangers, it is again formed into very small globules, and dried in the sun; broth of meat, or hot water, is then poured over it in a bowl. The bowl is placed in the middle of the floor.

The ladies, having carefully washed their hands, arranged themselves in a circle round the bowl, sitting on their heels. Mr. M. was directed to walk to and fro, and, as the ladies were anxious, as far as possible, to conceal their habits from European gentlemen, to cast his sight into the room without turning his head. Each lady helped herself by thrusting her hand into that part of the bowl nearest her, and, taking a small portion of its contents, pressed the fluid from it, and rolled it into a ball about the size of a nutmeg; then, extending her arm at full length, with surprising dexterity conveyed it into her mouth: not one that he saw missed her aim. To put the hand near the mouth when eating is considered a mark of vulgarity.

The ladies were natives of Senegal and Goree. Their property consisted of jewels and slaves, which they brought with them. Of jewels some of them have a profusion, which they are fond of exhibiting: they seldom burden themselves by carrying them, but a female slave sometimes walks before her mistress, heavily laden with rings of gold on her arms and legs, others stretching her ears, with chains and various trinkets hanging to her neck and other parts of her person.

The Missionaries preached to the Mandingoes through an interpreter; but soon found that they were likely, with the best interpreter they could find, to do more harm than good. Having acquired a smattering of the native language, they repeatedly detected errors in his translations. On one occasion, when the Missionary had been holding forth the superior benefits of Christianity as compared with Mohammedanism, the interpreter, in his zeal for the Missionary's cause, added, by saying, "*Beside that*, if you have a white man's religion you may drink rum." The Missionary interposed, saying, "What? Did you say Christians may get drunk?" "Yes," he replied; "me see plenty of white men drunk" (too true, no doubt).* From this time, until a young man was converted to God, they declined preaching through an interpreter.

* As the *Mohammedans* totally abstain from all intoxicating drinks, nothing is more disgusting to them than drunkenness.

FIRST-FRUITS OF THE GAMBIA MISSION, WEST AFRICA.

The little church at St. Mary's was visited weekly: the members continued stedfast, and proved themselves to be sincere in their professed love for the truth; yet it was some time before one of them professed to enjoy the witness of the Holy Spirit to their adoption into the family of God. On a Saturday evening a poor woman came to his lodgings in great anxiety, saying, "Massa, what me go do to be saved? That word Mr. Baker preached last Sunday cut my heart like one knife: me big sinner, pass every sinner in the world. What me go do massa?" After pointing her to the Saviour, he advised her to go home and pray until her trouble was taken away. The next morning, at seven o'clock, when he met the whole church together, she appeared with a cheerful countenance, indicating that she had prayed in faith. When asked the state of her mind, she replied, "Oh, massa! that time me left you last night, me go into the bush (the jungle), me put my knees on the ground and pray—pray long time—till all my troubles go away, and me glad too much."

"What make you so glad, Mary?"

"Massa, Jesus pardon my sins."

"How do you know that? Did any one tell you so?"

"Me don't know whether He speak or no; but," putting her hand upon her heart, she said, "it make so here: I feel em now."

"What did you do then?"

"Me can't pray no more, but me praise, me thank Massa Jesus for pardon."

"Have you not prayed since?"

"O, yes; me pray for pardon for my husband."

Her husband soon became a regular member of the congregation. This was regarded as the first-fruits of their industry, and was highly encouraging to them.

JUBILEE SONG.

O come, Eternal Spirit,
Tune our hearts to ecstacy,
Reveal what we inherit,
On this day of Jubilee.
Not to us, Lord, be the glory:
We are nothing in Thy sight;
'Tis the simple Gospel story
Which hath shed its glorious light.

'Tis the precious blood that pleadeth
For a lost and ruined race;
'Tis the Priest who intercedeth;
'Tis the spirit of all grace;
'Tis the hand that rolls the thunder;
'Tis the God all worlds obey,
Who alone hath wrought the wonders
Which we celebrate to-day.

Earthly vessels bore the treasure,
Human hands the seed hath sowed;
Even so, 'twas His good pleasure,
But the power was all of God.
After fifty years of blessing,—
Years with love and mercy fraught,—
We will praise Him without ceasing,
For the wonders He hath wrought.

He hath burst the bars of iron,
He hath set the captive free;
The mountains fled before Him,
He hath dried the swelling sea:
The wilderness is ringing
With our Redeemer's fame;
The distant isles are singing
The music of His name.

The Hindu temple shaketh,
Light gleams o'er China's wall,
Yea, Satan's kingdom quaketh,
And totters to its fall.
Our lives, and hearts, and voices,
Lord, join in praising Thee;
Yea, Heaven itself rejoices
In this our Jubilee.

THE

WESLEYAN JUVENILE OFFERING.

THE LITTLE GIRL

OF THE FROZEN LAND.

THE little girl of Greenland, or the frozen land, has a strange name; it is Equrk, and her brother is called Awahtok. They live with their parents in a low house, built of stones and plastered with moss, which looks like an old brick-oven. A house is called "*igloë*" in that country. It has but one room, and the people crawl into it through a low long passage on their hands and knees. Within, there is no fireplace, stove, or fire, nor a chair, table, or bed.

Equrk's father chiefly spends his time in fishing, and carries his canoe or boat on his back to the water; or, when the ice is too thick to break for fishing, he hunts the walrus.

How do you suppose Equrk's mother cooks her food? She boils it in a kettle over a lamp. The lamp is made of the shoulder-blade of a walrus, filled with blubber, with a wick of moss. As for baking, she never does that. Little Equrk never saw a slice of bread, or a potato, or an apple. She eats a steak of walrus, or some broiled blubber, or frozen liver; or she sucks a bear's paw, or the rib of a seal. Never a stick of sugar-candy had little Equrk. If you gave her one she would say, "Kuyanaka," which means "I thank you."

If Equrk goes out of doors, what does she see? green grass, and tulips, and buttercups? No. A corn-field over the way? No. Currant-bushes and cherry-trees, or oaks and elms branching overhead? No, no. On one side is a great ice-mountain, and fields of snow, snow, snow; nothing hardly but snow, with gray rocks here and there.

SUMMER IN THE FROZEN LAND.

A short time in the summer a little pale grass tries to grow in sunny spots, and a few small flowers smile by the gray rocks. Then the little girl must be happy indeed. She laughs, and has her games of play like you. She has no little carriage to run on the smooth ground; but her father makes her a sledge. He has no wood, for trees do not grow in that cold country;

so he takes the bones of the whale and the walrus, and fastens them together with seal-skin, and he makes a back to lean against, because it will go over some rather rough places. It runs very swiftly, for who do you think draws little Equrk? Not her father, he has gone hunting the great *nannook*, which is the white bear; not her brother Awahtok, he has his sledge; but a couple of little brown dogs, who are harnessed to the sledge: they run and draw Equrk, and very much does she enjoy the drive.

WHAT DRESS DOES SHE WEAR?

What does she dress in? Hood, and cloak, and gloves, like our little girls? I will begin with her feet. Nobody knits in that frozen land, so she has no warm *woollen* socks like yours. Her socks are made of bird-skins, with the soft down inside. Over this she wears seal-skin boots. These keep her feet warm. Then she wears leggings of white bear-skin, and a jacket of fox-skin. This jacket has a hood to it; and the garment, jacket, and hood together is called a jumper. That is the fashion of that country. It would look odd enough in our land. At first sight you would take little Equrk for a stray cub of the white bear. Sometimes she holds a fox's bushy tail between her teeth to keep Jack Frost from kissing her cheeks with his cold lips.

Oh! you do not know what terrible winters she sees in her country. The sun sets in November, and it does not rise again till March. Think what a long night that is. We think winter days are short enough; but to have no day at all, how much worse that is! There are the northern lights to be sure, but there is no light like the bright, warm, cheerful sun which we see in our sky.

SOWING AND REAPING.

"They that sow in tears shall reap in joy."

THE Missionaries in the Friendly and Fiji Islands had many trials, and dangers to pass through when they went to preach the Gospel to the heathen, and to the cruel cannibals who lived there. You have heard of some of these trials: they did indeed "sow in tears:" but after a time came their reward: thousands of the natives were converted, and became good Christians. Many died rejoicing in God, and the good work still goes on: the joyful reaping-time is not over, as you will see from accounts which have been sent home by Mr. Langham, in Fiji, and Mr. Davis, in the Friendly Islands, of the happy deaths of Christian believers.

The old Fijian woman.

A poor old Fijian woman was thought to be dying. "I asked her," said the Missionary, "the state of her mind in the prospect of death." She said, "Oh my chief, I am so happy: my sins are forgiven. God's anger is taken away; I am one of God's children. He loves me, and I love Him. I am not afraid to die, because I know I shall go to be with my Saviour. God is so good to me: when I pray to Him He hears me, He comes to me: indeed, He is never away from me, He is always near me. O my chief, my soul does rejoice in my Saviour."

The dying Fiji scholar.

A child from the day-school, about twelve years of age, died, saying, "I am Christ's, I am Christ's."

The poor Fijian believer.

I visited a poor man who was stretched upon his mat to die. With broken utterance he said, "I have no friend but Jesus: my earthly friends have all left me, but Jesus loves me still. There is no love like my Saviour's. He does not forsake me when I am helpless and dying."

The Christian convert in the Friendly Islands.

Some time since I attended one of our earliest converts, who was fully expecting to finish his course of labour and suffering; and when asked what were his prospects in reference to the future, he replied, "I have no fear of death. The blood of Christ has washed away my sins, and I feel as if I were on board a vessel, with its sails spread, and a good breeze, and every prospect of speedily arriving at the port."

ALL THE ISLES OF
THE HEATHEN
SHALL WORSHIP HIM.

ZEPHANIAH ii. 11.

A MANDINGO TOWN IN WESTERN AFRICA.

A Missionary being desirous of seeing the natives of Western Africa under their own Government, visited Cape St. Mary, where there is a Mandingo town.

The town, in the distance, appeared like a number of stacks of clover, with the thatch turned black; but on entering, he found these stacks swarming, not with rats or mice, but with men, women, and naked children, blacker than their habitations.

In the middle of the huts, in an open place, sat the chief, or headman, teaching a number of boys the Arabic alphabet, the characters being burnt on a board. The old chief rose at the approach of the white men, bowed politely, and cordially shook hands with them. Such politeness among naked savages surprised the stranger: he learnt that it came to them, from an Arabian source, with the Mohammedan religion.

The natives were fond of compliments, and liked to be told that they looked large. To say to one of those black gentlemen, "You are like a bull, Sir," or "You are like an elephant, Sir," would be highly gratifying. The old Mohammedan chief he then saw, in bulk and shape, appeared almost as much like a bull as a man.

The Missionary spent the night in a hut assigned him by the chief. It was badly furnished for a man fresh from England, but it served as a pretty fair seasoning for a young Missionary.

For the bed there was nothing but a rack of sticks laid across each other, resting on four forked stakes. He lay all night sleepless, longing for the morning.

As soon as the daylight returned he walked forth from his hut to the edge of a cliff, where he saw the river, and the brig at anchor from which he had lately landed. While looking at the vessel, his doubts and fears respecting the natives induced a feeling of deep regret that he could not, consistently with his duty to those who sent him there, return immediately to the ship, and back to England.

Before eight o'clock he received a message from the kind old chief to breakfast with him, and a nice-looking bowl of boiled white rice, with a boiled fowl upon it, was placed on the ground to be eaten, but neither knife, fork, or spoon appeared, nor had he any thing of the kind with him. But the chief soon showed the white man the most simple and expeditious way of using the food, by thrusting his hand into the rice, and raising it, fully charged, to his mouth, inviting his guest to follow his example, by saying, "Come, Tobaub" (white-man), "eat."

A sharp appetite helped the Englishman to overcome his European objections. But a greater difficulty remained: How is the fowl to be divided? His friend, however, soon enlightened him on this point also, by laying hold of one leg, and directing him to seize the other, when a gentle pull gave each a leg for his own mouth. Having eaten this, each got a wing by the same process. Then, using both hands, he divided the body with equal ease. The delicacy of the Missionary's stomach was somewhat relieved by having observed that the Mohammedans carefully wash their hands before they eat.

A HINDOO PRINCE GOING TO PAY A VISIT.

This is a curious picture, dear children. The man in the palki is an Indian rajah, or prince, and appears to be going out to pay a visit to some friend of his, probably another rajah; hence the highly ornamental palki, or carriage, he has chosen, and which he intends his fellow rajah should admire; he seems, too, to have made himself very comfortable in it.

You would be amused at the drawing-room duty he and his friend will perform. As soon as he approaches the gates of his friend's house, his bearers (who are the men bearing his palki) will set up a shout, to the effect that the "great rajah of such and such a place is coming." Then the other rajah's servants (many of whom are sure to be lazily lolling about in the verandahs) will immediately bestir themselves, and shout the same thing to each other with as much fuss as possible.

When the palki stops at the gate, they will very officiously assist his highness to get out, holding a large white cotton umbrella over him, and pretending to brush away any little specks of dust that may be in the way. He will then be ushered into the room, where he will take a chair, and sit with his legs crossed under him on it. Should there be no chair, he will just as complacently assume the same position on the floor. Then his friend will come in, finely dressed, to show *he* can be grand too. They won't shake hands, but they will sit opposite to each other, a good distance apart, smoking hookahs for about a couple of hours, scarcely saying any thing. Then, if the bearers have sufficiently rested, the visitor has his palki once more brought round to the door, and, "hoping that his friends' shadow may never grow less," he takes himself off, and is once more shouted out of the place, congratulating himself while on his way home upon the very lively morning he has spent.

A CHAPTER ABOUT THE KARENS.

I DARE say many readers of the "Juvenile Offering" have heard of the Karens, a people who are scattered over various parts of Burmah and Siam, and who, in former days, were so cruelly oppressed by the Burmese Government, that they were compelled to fly for protection to the mountains and jungles, where they took up their abode, and where great numbers remain to the present day.

These people are not idolaters, but have always retained a knowledge of the true God, though mixed up with sinful and degrading superstitions.

They had an ancient prophecy transmitted to them from their forefathers, which declared that when their misery was at its height, white foreigners would come from the West, deliver them from their oppressors, and teach them the true religion; so that, when they heard of the British soldiers landing in Burmah, they said, "These are our deliverers;" and truly enough they were; for the country falling under English rule, they were entitled to the same protection as all other subjects of our beloved Queen; and being able, without fear of persecution, to attend to the instruction of the white foreigners (Missionaries), great numbers embraced Christianity.

During a recent visit to Rangoon we were greatly

interested in visiting the schools, and in listening to the statements of Missionaries respecting their former misery and degradation; and when we thought of the wretchedness of their past life, it was very pleasant to see them looking so happy, and to hear them sing beautiful hymns descriptive of the blessedness of religion, and the happiness of a future state.

In their heathen state they are so superstitious, that if a white bird—called a rice bird—should happen to settle on any part of a house, the inhabitants would desert it immediately, believing that dreadful calamities would overtake them should they remain. Houses may frequently be met with that have been forsaken in this way.

They devote their attention almost exclusively to the cultivation of rice and vegetables; but if a small animal, somewhat resembling a rabbit, were to cross a rice field, the owner dare not retain it in his possession, being firmly persuaded that if he did so all his family would die. Mr. Brayton mentioned the case of a man who possessed a field of rice, and, when it was just ready to be reaped, one of these innocent little creatures had the misfortune to run over it. The poor man was in despair, for himself and family were entirely dependent on this rice field, but he dare not reap it, and was preparing to abandon it and seek subsistence elsewhere, when a happy thought struck Mr. B., and he immediately went to a Karen Christian who had a field of rice ready for the sickle, and, explaining to him how matters stood, asked if he would be willing to make an exchange.

The Christian Karen pitied the poor man, for he himself had been a slave to the same superstition, and readily agreed to take the field in exchange for his own, to the great joy of the latter, who was, nevertheless, astonished that his friend should be willing to incur such an awful risk. But when the field was reaped, and none of the expected calamities befel the reaper, the Karen was so struck with the fact, that he, with his family, renounced his superstitions, and embraced Christianity.

During the dry season it is customary for the Missionaries to sail along the numerous rivers which intersect the country, and visit the villages which are scattered on their banks.

Mrs. B. informed us, that during one of these excursions they came to a village where she was accosted by an aged woman, who expressed an ardent desire to know about Jesus Christ and the doctrines of Christianity. Mrs. B. gladly complied with her request, and, with a full and grateful heart, told her of the Saviour coming into the world to die for sinners, and how all the wretched sinful children of men, of every colour and in every clime, might, through Him, obtain pardon and peace here, and heaven hereafter. While she was speaking, the poor woman fixed her eyes on her, and eagerly drank in every word. "Oh," said she, "how I have longed to see you! I heard of you last year, but when I arrived at the village you had gone. I followed a long way in a boat, but could not overtake you. Oh, mamma, I have one great sorrow in my heart. I have lost my husband and five children: they died, all of them, and left me alone and desolate. My heart is full of sorrow. Tell me, can Jesus Christ cure a great sorrow?" She listened joyfully to the story of the good Physician who could heal the broken heart, and who never refused any that applied to him for relief; and as Mrs. B. explained the doctrines of Christianity she embraced them with earnestness, and the simplicity of a child.

After they have lost any friends it is customary

to hold a feast for the dead, where many sinful and superstitious rites are practised. They were preparing to hold it on the following day, but, on being told that if she embraced Christianity she must abandon such sinful practices, the feast was given up, and she expressed her desire to follow the wishes of the Missionary in every thing. The following year she was one of the first to welcome them to the village. They found that she, and most of her relatives, all aged people, had embraced Christianity. They were then admitted into the Christian church by baptism; and this once poor, miserable creature exclaimed, "Oh, mamma, I am sure now that Jesus Christ can cure one great sorrow, for He has cured mine."

Mamma is a title they use in addressing the ladies connected with the Mission.

CHRIST AS A SAVIOUR.

DEAR children, commit yourselves to Jesus as your Saviour. He is *mighty* to save. What encouragement! He is *willing* to save. More encouragement still! He *waits* to save. He stretches out his hand all the day long. He is ready to save *now*.

Are you ready to ask him to save? May the Holy Spirit enable you to cry and pray, "Lord, save—Lord, save me from sin, from Satan, from hell. Oh, save me now!" If you pray thus with the heart, he will hear your prayer; he will come and save. "He will gather you with his arms, and carry you in his bosom."

Children's Bible Hymn.

Music by R. H. MILES.

Book of hope! the spirit, sighing,
Consolation finds in thee,
As it hears the Saviour crying,
"Come, come to Me."

Book of peace! when nights of sorrow
Fall upon us drearily,
Thou wilt bring a shining morrow,
Full, full of thee.

SPRING THOUGHTS.

Upon our youthful way,
  Hope's fairy blossoms lie;
Though cloud and sun alternate play
  Upon life's changeful sky,
Yet are they April shadows bright,
With borderings of sunny light.

But all these smiles of spring
  Must shine and pass away;
For time fleets by with noiseless wing,
  And day succeedeth day;
And spring will all be over soon,
And life's young morning reach its noon.

If in the spring-time bright
  No blossoms grace the tree,
How shall the autumn's mellow light
  A golden fruitage see?
How, if no precious seed we sow,
Shall we a joyous harvest know?

Lord! in life's morning hour
  We bring our hearts to Thee;
As dew upon the opening flower,
  So let Thy blessings free,
Thy tender love, Thy watchful care,
Fall on our hearts, and linger there.

And help us, then, to tell
  The mercy we have found;
As that fair-blossom'd dew-filled bell
  Sheds a sweet odour round,
So we, as little flowers, would bloom,
And fill earth's garden with perfume.

E. M. S.

THE

WESLEYAN JUVENILE OFFERING.

THE MISSIONARY AND HIS INTERPRETER IN WESTERN AFRICA.

In the picture you see two preachers and two congregations: the reason is, the Missionary did not know the language of the country, so he got an interpreter to help him. A few of the people understand a little

English. The Missionary and the interpreter stand back to back: those who understand English are before the Missionary, the others sit in front of the interpreter. The Missionary begins slowly, with half a sentence at a time, and then waits till the interpreter has translated it: then a whole sentence. But he soon finds that his friend is getting on before him: the interpreter is so eager to tell the good news of the Gospel, that he cannot wait for the Missionary, but, with lifted hands and earnest voice, tells his countrymen what he knows about Christ.

THE KING OF QUINELLA.

I will tell you something about one of the kings of this country that the Missionary paid a visit to.

The king, being informed that a white man wished to see him, gave him permission to approach the royal presence.

The outside wall of the palace, of hard wrought earth, formed a circle about twenty feet in diameter, and three feet and a half high; in the centre of that was another circular wall, about six feet high; a roof of bamboo canes, tapering to a cone, and thatched with long grass, rested on these walls. A hole under the eaves answered the double purpose of doorway and chimney. To enter, he had to creep: in the centre he could stand erect. The centre was the chief sleeping-room, and had in it a constant fire, which was kept chiefly to supply smoke to drive away mosquitos.

Conducted through the centre, the white man was led to the outer circle, where the king sat on the earth floor, reclining against the inner wall. Some of his chiefs were seated with him. The principal mark of distinction between the king and those about him was a piece of dirty scarlet cloth on his head. As a mark of respect, his majesty ordered a log of wood to be placed by his side, as a seat for the white stranger, and politely held out his hand, and gave that of the white man a hearty shake. The Missionary then laid his present at the king's feet, which was thankfully received. The following conversation ensued—

"I am glad to see you," said the king: "I want to see plenty of white men in my country."

Missionary.—"I am not come to your country to trade, but am sent by good men in my country, to whom the great Creator of the world has given a book which makes known his will concerning them, and you, and all men in every part of the world. To make it known to you I am come to learn your language, and to give you that book in your own language, that you and your children may be wise and happy as we are."

King—"That is *very good;* but don't you want gold, slaves, wax, nor hides?"

Missionary—"I want nothing of that at all: I only want the king to give a place to build my house, that myself and my brother may live among you, and teach you and your children that good way."

King—"That is very good—*too good:* take the land as much as you want, and where you please; but I advise you to build your house near the river, that if my people attempt to injure you, you might jump into a canoe and get out of their reach. (This certainly was kind on the king's part, but not very comforting to the Missionary.)

Missionary—"I do not know how grants of land are secured among you. The king's word will doubtless be sufficient during his life; but the next king may deny the white man's claim to the land."

At this the whole company burst into a roar of laughter.

"What are they laughing at?" said the Missionary.

"They are laughing at you," said the interpreter. "You must not mention death in the presence of the king. The king never dies. He will be pleased if you say you hope he will live a thousand years."

The white man, as a stranger, obtained an excuse for a great breach of court etiquette, which would have subjected a native to a broken head.

Say among the heathen that the Lord reigneth.

PSALM xcvi. 10.

MISSIONARY DIFFICULTIES.

A WATCH-NIGHT WITHOUT A CLOCK OR WATCH, AND A TEA-PARTY WITHOUT CUPS AND SAUCERS.

THESE are Mr. and Mrs. Sinclair's difficulties. They live in that far-distant country, Hudson's Bay. Mr. Sinclair says, in a letter to me—"We are going to have our watch-night the last night of the year, but neither watch or clock is there in the whole station. Two years ago I was going on a Missionary tour with Mr. McDougal, and we were capsized in a rapid, and my watch was spoiled."

Travelling in these countries is often done in canoes on the river. Sometimes the river falls down a steep place, making a little water-fall or rapid. When these falls are not too steep, the traveller will go down in the canoe: this is called shooting a rapid. Sometimes the canoe is upset, as Mr. Sinclair was. I dare say he was obliged to swim for his life, for he would be in danger of being drowned. When these rapids are too steep for them to venture down in the canoe, the travellers have to get out, unload their canoe, and carry goods and canoe too by the side of the river to the bottom of the fall, put their boat into the river again, replace their goods, and go on: rather a tedious way of travelling, I think.

Mrs. Sinclair's difficulty is this. She says, "We are going to have a tea-party on New-year's day, but we have so few cups and saucers, there will not be nearly enough for all the Indians and their wives that will come."

In that country the frost is very severe: cups and saucers, and all kinds of crockery, break very soon. In England, in frosty weather, glasses and cups break more readily than in the summer: of course, in cold, cold Hudson's Bay it is much worse, where it freezes so hard, that if you take hold of the iron latch of the door it will blister your fingers as if they were burnt, and where you have milk sent to you frozen, wrapped in a rabbit skin, as poor Mrs. Brooking once told us she had.

How Mrs. Sinclair managed her tea-party without cups and saucers I do not know, for her letter was sent off before the day it was to be held. I think we must try and send some cups and saucers to her, and perhaps we might get a clock or a watch for Mr. Sinclair.

A JUBILEE HYMN.

HAIL to the Jubilee!
  Loud let the trumpet sound
And let it echoed be,
  The earth's wide circuit round,
The joyful tidings to proclaim,
The world shall hear the Saviour's name!

We sing of triumphs past,
  Mid heathen nations wrought,
And toward the future cast
  Full many a prayerful thought:
But hark! the trump of Jubilee,
Foretells a mightier victory.

The toil of fifty years,
  Doth a rich harvest yield,
And they who sow in tears
  Shall reap the fruitful field;
But wider shall the seed be cast,
And golden sheaves exceed the past.

Hail, year of Jubilee!
  God of the infant church,
We glory give to Thee,
  While we the records search,
And wondering see whose mighty hand
Hath thus increased the little band!

Yes ! 'tis Thy power alone
Such wonders hath achieved,
Our fathers' God we own,
In whom we have believed ;
And wilt thou not in this our day
Again revive that power, we pray ?

O ! let the Jubilee
A Pentecost become ;
The Church looks up to Thee,
Prepares to make Thee room,
And breathes the universal cry,
" Send down the Spirit from on high."

Thy servants, Lord, accept,
Their vows and offerings new,
Who solemnly have kept
Thy former deeds in view ;
Each heart afresh with grace baptize,
And thus approve the sacrifice.

Maintain thy cause, O Lord,
O'er all the earth maintain,
Till all shall hear Thy word,
And life through Jesus gain ;
Then loud the mighty hymn shall swell
Of praise to our Emmanuel. F. W.

SOWING IN TEARS.

Last month we told you, dear children, of the joyful reaping of the Missionaries in Fiji, in witnessing the happy deaths of the old and young Fijian Christians.

This picture gives you another scene—Mrs. Hunt watching by the side of her dying child. The child is sick unto death, and the mother is sitting weeping by its side, when she is disturbed by noises at the window, and, looking up, she sees, to her sorrow and dismay, fierce Fijian faces looking in at her, jeering and mocking at her sorrow.

Mr. and Mrs. Hunt had not been long among these Fijians, who were heathens and cannibals. They did not want the Gospel, and they did not love the Missionaries, and they would have liked to have eaten Mrs. Hunt and her child too, if God had not restrained their rage.

And so the poor mother sits alone with her child, no kind neighbour looking in to comfort and help her: black, scowling Fijians are her neighbours.

The baby died, and the greatest grief of the mother seemed to be that her child would be buried in that heathen land, where the very ground seemed cursed through the wickedness of the people; but she would not have been sorry to have laid her babe in Fiji soil if she had known what she knows now; that from God's blessing on the labours of her husband and his fellow-Missionaries, and the faith and love of their wives, when her babe shall arise on the morning of the resurrection, tens of thousands of rejoicing Fijians will rise with it to bless God to all eternity for having sent the Missionaries to them. The dear babe was buried in the garden, and the king, whose heart God in mercy had softened, sent some of his carpenters to build a house over his grave. This was the sowing time.—The Missionaries cast in the precious seeds, and watched and prayed, and hoped to see the precious fruits; but the harvest was not to be yet: the heathen raged fearfully.

One day a great savage, in a flaming passion, flung open the Mission-house door, crying out, "I am very angry." He then seized Mr. Hunt and Mr. Lyth, one in each hand, and threw them to the door, where he had left his club, intending to kill them. But God took care of his servants, and the chief let them go, striking Mr. Lyth on the face as he went away.

After this, Mrs. Lyth's child died, and they buried him in the little house where Mrs. Hunt's baby was laid. Still the heathen rage. The Mission ship "Triton" was coming to bring them their letters from home, and supplies of food, which they could not get in Fiji. When the ship got near the island she missed her proper course, and was making direct for the rocks, where she was sure to be wrecked. The savages rejoiced and grew wild with excitement, and made sure of a rich prize. The wives of the Missionaries heard them say they would fasten them up in their houses, and then came a mad shout as the ship struck on the coral reef, and the crowd, with fierce cries and whirling of clubs, rushed to the shore to begin their work of murder and plunder. One of the wives went aside, looked up, and prayed, "Almighty Jesus, we need thy help." She arose, and the prayer was answered. When she looked out the "Triton" was gently gliding into deep water before the savages could reach her.

SWARTZ, THE GERMAN MISSIONARY.

SWARTZ was born in Prussia in 1726. He had a good mother, who often prayed over him, and brought him up in the fear and love of God; and when she lay on her death-bed, she told her husband and pastor that she had given her son up to the service of God, and begged them to carry out her wishes as far as they could. While he was studying at college, a good man proposed to him that he should begin to learn Tamil, one of the languages of India, that he might help to translate the Bible into that language. This work made him think about the millions of poor heathen who had no one to teach them the blessed Gospel; and as he grew older, and loved the Saviour more, he began to feel how much he should like to go and work among them. He knew there were a few Missionaries in India, and they wanted help very much; so when he was twenty-three years of age he dutifully told his father of his wishes. His father took three days to consider, and then bade him go forth in God's name, and be faithful unto death in the good work he had chosen. Like Xavier, he began with the little ones. He would gather the "young lambs" around him, and teach them about Jesus. When he knew the language better, he began to teach and preach to the grown-up people, and they flocked round him in numbers to hear his words. The Hindoos used to call him "Father," he was so kind and good to them; and many who would not attend to his preaching, were won to Christ by his holy, loving life. He laboured for years amongst them, never thinking of himself, and the people loved and reverenced him, and his preaching was blessed to hundreds of them, who became Christians, and whose descendants are Christians to this day.

THE HISTORY OF A HINDOO GOD.

"IN a large room of a temple I went to visit," says a Missionary, "are two large granite idols, the one on the left hand is the 'god of obstacles.' This is his history. He was the son of Siva and Parvathi. When he was a baby, Parvathi made him her door-keeper, and one day the god Humara, who had long entertained a grudge against him, found him alone, and cut off his head. Siva was very sorry when he heard of it, and vowed that he would replace his head with the head of the first living thing that he should find lying down with his head to the north. He started off to look, but unfortunately the first thing he came to in that position was an elephant; but, true to his vow, he chopped off the elephant's head, and hurried home, and clapped it on to the neck of his son, and restored him to life.

His mother, Parvathi, was terribly frightened when she first saw him in this condition, but finally got used to him, and did not mind the change. But the poor fellow never could get married; for though he hunted the world over, he never could find a woman who would marry such a monster. He was a great glutton.

He is one of the most universally adored gods of India, and the reason they all worship him is because they are afraid of him. I said before that he is the god of obstacles. So when they are going to have a feast, or a wedding, or any public ceremony, or when a man is going to start on a pilgrimage, or begin any important matter, they worship him, so that he will not hinder them in any way in what they are trying to do. His image is found everywhere—in temples, rest-houses in groves, by tanks and wells, and by the side of the road, and in the private houses. Everywhere you see the elephant trunk-nosed god.

In this temple he has tumbled down on his back, and there he lies, for, poor fellow! he cannot pick himself up, and no one dares touch him to pick him up, for fear it will kill him to touch him. What they are going to do about it I do not know. I do not think, however, that you would be afraid to pick him up, would you? But you would have to lift very hard, for he is solid granite, and very heavy.

THE PAPER OF WARNING.

BY MARTIN ZIUGASTOR.

THIS account is sent to you, my young friends, by a Missionary's wife who lives at the Mission station in South Africa, where the Kaffir boy, of whom she tells you, died. The English in which it is written will seem strange to you, and you will think it is not as we talk in this country: the account was written by a Kaffir youth in his own language, and Mrs. Bertram has translated it by just putting the Kaffir words into English, and has not altered the sentences.

"I send you the following account of a native youth about sixteen years of age, on his death bed; written by one of his companions in the Kaffir language, which I will translate for the "Juvenile Offering."

MARTIN'S ACCOUNT.

"It was so when he was sick, that he one day called his mother into his bedroom, and said to her, 'Send the children to prayer-meeting.' Again he said to his mother this thing, 'I fear that the children do not go to the prayer-meeting on the Sabbath morning;' at the same time inquiring where his brother was, saying, 'These are they I am so constantly trying to awaken. Is my brother still there?' Again he said, 'I fear that thing, that the children, when they are awoke, will not rise and go to the prayer-meeting; on the Sabbath-day, ever since I read a book that talked so nicely to me and to you, my brother, I give this book to you often to read, and tell you it is a nice book.' After they had all left for the prayer-meeting, he repeated some very pretty lines of a Kaffir hymn. 'The day of the Sabbath has again appeared. 'Tis a day of great rejoicing. 'Tis a day that believers long for the place they are going to.'

"Early on the Monday he expressed a wish to see all his friends. They soon came; but when he saw them all he was much affected, feeling very happy in Christ, and began to address them on the subject of religion; but his cough being very troublesome, they advised him to refrain from much speaking, as his chest was so bad. In the evening some young men went in to see him. He requested them to come forward to the light, that he might see them.

"He began to speak these words—'This earth is not ours. We were a number that went to learn to work at the Institution, also to be taught the word of God; but to-day you see what I am. It is well that you see me this day as I am, because you will also be brought to this; but my heart looks to the Lord. Think, then, that to you also are coming such days as these: therefore, then, try at once to pray that you might find peace. Perhaps you may never see me again.'

"On the Wednesday his father went into his bed-room, and he asked his father what his feelings were: if he had given him up. His father, in reply, said that he had given him up freely some days ago, when he was so ill, but seeing him slightly better he had asked the Lord to lend him his son again. He then said, 'Why have you asked for me?' The father said, 'Because of the morning and evening prayer.' He then said, 'It must not be only evening and morning prayer, my father, but at night, when you awake on your bed: at *all* times lift up your heart to God. And this that you ask of God, what is it? What kind of child am I, that you make such a request?' His father answered, 'Because you are a good child.' He then said to his father, 'I am a child still, and little in heart, and not grown so as to reach his full stature; yes, still, still I am in the service, although I am not born anew in the Lord.' His father then asked him what he had been doing so long. Then he replied, 'I have been praying, and even now, this night, I have great hope.' Soon after this all retired to rest.

About midnight his father, heard him call out loudly, 'Father, arise and light the candle.' His father was soon by his side with a light and looking over him greatly agitated, because he thought his dear son was or had already taken leave of him; but at the moment of his bending over him the son exclaimed, 'Father,' throwing his arms around his neck, 'my good father, don't be alarmed, but let me greet you. The Lord has greatly blessed me with His Holy Spirit. In my soul I am born anew. I have great joy in my soul.' The father then said, 'My son has listened to the throbbings of my heart. All fear has vanished: joy is mine:' and, turning to his wife, said, 'Let us kneel down to thank God for this.' The next day he said he was still happy; yes, the same as he had told his Missionary the day before. Soon after this, on Sunday, 1st November, about two o'clock, his spirit took its flight into the land of everlasting bliss." Mrs. Bertram says:—" I might add that his sufferings were great, and he was long on the bed of affliction, but throughout the whole of the same he manifested much patience, and was never heard to murmur.

" We may learn much from such scenes of affliction, for verily the word of God is powerful, testifying its great might and wondrous power even in the retired dwelling of the once benighted heathen of South Africa."

Lessington, November 11, 1863. G. BERTRAM.

THE

WESLEYAN JUVENILE OFFERING.

LITTLE ANNIE;

THE MISSIONARY'S CHILD WHO DIED AT CAPE TOWN, SOUTH AFRICA.

ANNIE HARDEY was born about the month of May 1860, at Perth, in Western Australia. When she was two years old her father removed to Cape Town.

By the winning ways of childhood, and a peculiar sweetness of disposition, she, the youngest of the family, won the affection of all. She proved a little sunbeam, gladdening every heart and brightening every path with which she had to do. But her ministry was soon completed. When but three years and eight months of age, God, in his providence, afflicted her with bronchitis, of which she died December 25th, 1863.

Some weeks before her death she was overheard saying to her brother James, two years older than herself, "Perhaps I shall not live till the bazaar, James. I am not going to live long. I shall die; and you can ask papa to let you come and look into my grave. But don't cry: only my body will be there; my spirit will be with the angels in heaven." On another occasion she said to her sister Eliza, "I shall *die* after the bazaar."

Several times, on different occasions, she said, "Mamma, when are we going to heaven?" or, "When is God going to take us to heaven?" as if thinking she and her mother were going together. A few Sundays before her illness, Annie sat upon the sofa, by her mother, and said, "Mamma, what is *save?*" It was explained; and when her mother, proceeding to speak of the death of Jesus, said, "He died to save *you* from dying," Annie evidently understood the saying, and tears moistened her eyes.

Shortly after the bazaar above alluded to, she was seized with a cold, and on Sunday morning, December 20th, the doctor was called in. When he had gone, she said, "Mamma, let *us* go to chapel. I am quite well enough." She was told it would be better to stay at home. When left alone with her mother, Annie said, "Mamma, sing the hymn 'Thy will be done.'" Her mother hesitated, and Annie said again, "Sing 'Thy will be done,'" and her request was complied with. Never before had she been known to ask for this hymn, but several times during this day she repeated this request. Afterwards not a day passed but she wished to hear the strains of that tune and hymn. The following Wednesday her eldest sister, who had been from home, returned. No others being present, Annie, sitting on her sister's lap, said, "Mary Ann, sing 'Thy will be done.'" Her sister, not having heard her ask for it before, proposed to sing something else, which she had been fond of hearing. "No," said Annie, "that is the one I like best."

At another time, when suffering from a blister on the neck, she said, "Oh my neck," and immediately asked for "Thy will be done." The following Friday (Christmas-day), towards the evening, when all hope of her recovery was failing, her mother asked, "Annie, is

Jesus near you?" "Yes." "Does Jesus love you?" "Yes." "Do you love Jesus?" "Yes." Anxious to know more, her mother said, "Annie, what did Jesus die to do?" "To save *me* from dying," was the distinct and unhesitating reply. The mother, rejoicing in heart, spoke of the love of Jesus, and, quoting the words of our Saviour, "Suffer little children to come unto me, and forbid them not, for of such is the kingdom of heaven," added, "He will take care of *you*, and take *you* in his arms, dear Annie." The little one replied, "Say 'I think when I read that sweet story of old." Her eldest sister repeated it. "Say it again." Again it was given. After a short pause, her mother said to her, "Annie, who did Jesus die to save?" "Me," was the emphatic reply. "Are you happy, Annie?" An impressive "Oh yes," was twice given, the second time sinking into a murmur. "Annie, would you like the angels to take you?" "*Not yet.*" "But you would like to see Jesus, dear?" "*Yes.*"

The same evening Annie asked her papa to sing "Gentle Jesus," and her mamma "Thy will be done," but before they could finish them Annie appeared too exhausted to listen, and said, "I think that is enough." Half an hour after midnight she was seized with two convulsive fits, followed by unconsciousness, until half-past one, when she gently breathed her last.

Thus departed little Annie, who, by her continual requests, taught her parents submission to the divine will, fulfilled her short mission on earth, and then sweetly slept in Jesus.

IN MEMORY OF LITTLE ANNIE, TO HER LITTLE BROTHER JAMES; SENT ON THE DAY OF ANNIE'S FUNERAL.

I had a little sister here,
A lovely, darling child,
Whose eyes were ever bright and clear,
Her temper was so mild.

She was too pure a gem to stay,
Where sin pollutes the air
So God has taken her away
To yonder world so fair.

She lives in heaven, where angels dwell,
And sees her Saviour's face;
And listens while the angels tell
The glories of the place.

And little Annie looks so white,
Amongst the happy throng,
And wears a crown so sparkling bright,
And sings the angels' song.

They tell her of their happy home,
And of their Maker's love;
And say they're very glad she's come,
To dwell with them above.

They point to earth, and show her where
Her friends and kindred are.
She loves us now, though dwelling there,
Away so very far.

She has a harp, and learns to play
Upon the tuneful strings.
Oh, how I long to fly away,
And hear the song she sings.

Thousands of little children meet
In raptures round the throne,
And Jesus smiles, and looks so sweet,
And calls them all his own.

He loves them all, and knows them well,
And says these jewels are mine;
Beside me they shall ever dwell,
And in my crown shall shine.

Papa! mamma! Oh do not weep,
Dear Annie shines with them:
God gave her not for us to keep,
He only lent the gem.

By Mrs. Morgan.

TRAVELLING IN WESTERN AFRICA.

In Western Africa the sky, during seven months of the year, is bright and cloudless; but the heat by day is intolerable. By night the temperature is pleasant, but you are tormented by mosquitoes and other insects; and your rest is disturbed by the noise of ferocious beasts, ranging the woods in search of their prey. The roaring of the lion, the snarling of the leopard, the screaming of the hyena, the barking of the wolf, make the traveller sometimes doubt the safety of his resting-place; but if a fire is kept burning near the spot, there is not much danger to be apprehended, except from large serpents. These will not scruple silently to creep into the hut.

A Missionary was once in a doorless negro's hut, endeavouring to sleep on a bundle of grass, having his feet uncovered and on the floor. In the middle of the night he heard nothing, but felt that some reptile took his great toe into its mouth, and drew its teeth softly over the skin, which caused him to start up ; but, as it was dark, he saw nothing. But about the same hour of the next night a black sentinel saw by moonlight a large serpent, thirteen feet long, close by the doorway of the hut, and killed it with the butt-end of his musket.

By day the cooling stream under the shade of a tree presents a strong temptation to the lover of a bath ; but let him take care that a crocodile, from twenty to thirty feet long, be not watching to devour him.

On the river, your right to advance is disputed by monkeys occupying the trees bordering the stream. Sometimes they become outrageous ; climbing the trees, chattering in the most menacing tones, breaking off sticks, and throwing them with all their might, bending the extreme branches, and shaking them at their enemies ; thus broadly intimating what they would do, if the water did not prevent their near approach.

GIVING UP ALL FOR CHRIST.

Did you ever hear the story of the North-American Indian and the Missionary? The Indian wanted to be a Christian. The Missionary said he must give up all for Christ, and then he would be a Christian. "Well," said he, "I give up my blanket." "No ; that is not enough." "I give up my gun." "Not enough yet." "I give up my dog." "More yet." The Indian dropped his head and wept. He had nothing else to give. "Are you sure that is all?" At last he said, "I give myself to Him." "Aye, that will do."

THE HAPPY CHILDREN.

A Missionary's wife in Burmah has written a nice story about her schoolchildren, which I am sure you will like to hear. She says—

"The kind friend who has built us the chapel has made a small room for me on one end, close by the river, and I was sitting there whilst the chapel was being swept, thinking of these changes, when familiar sounds fell upon my ear; and, as I went into the chapel, the scene was before me. Ah! it was not the sound of heathen revellers. It was the teacher and the school from one of our stations, who had come to spend the Sabbath with us. On they came in their little canoes, with the dip and the splash of their little oars, while little voices swelled the sweet song of 'Happy land.' They changed their garments on the bank of the river, and then the little company of forty came to greet me. I asked some of the children, who were not over nine years of age, if they were not very tired after the long run. 'Oh, no,' they replied; 'we sang almost all the way, and it did not seem like work.' After a little while I called them all together, and they repeated the catechism, commandments, and the Lord's Prayer, &c.

"One little bright-eyed boy came very close to me, and when I asked him what he desired, he said, 'Oh, nothing, only I want to say we are happy: we don't say bad words any more, and we know that God is with us. As I smiled upon the little fellow, they whispered to each other, and then many of them joined the little boy, and said they were very happy."

HOME DUTIES.

PRAYER.

It is "long, long ago," dear children, since we had our last talk about home duties, and agreed (some of us at least) to set apart a little time every day to pray for Missionaries and their work. Have we done it? For our little band I can say yes; and can add that, after a few months' trial, they mean to persevere, for they find it good. And now the next thing we ask you is, to be little "Methodists," in praying for Missions—Methodists in the sense in which the name was first given to Mr. Wesley and his friends; that is, have a *method*. Most of you have heard of the week of prayer at the beginning of the year, when Christians all over

the world pray for the same things on the same day. Now it is something like this we mean; for instance, how would this do?—

Sabbath. Our native land and the Jews.
Monday. Europe and its islands.
Tuesday. Africa and its islands.
Wednesday. Asia and its islands.
Thursday. North America and its islands.
Friday. South America and its islands.
Saturday. Australia, Polynesia, and the wide wide sea.

Of course the same places coming each week the year round, would leave plenty of room for subdivision. For instance, take the first. One week it might be England, another Scotland, another Ireland, another the Isle of Man and the other islands round the coasts. The Jews we can follow all over the earth, and pray for them in many different aspects.

Then, if we read much about Missions, we shall always have something special to pray for. A Mr. Champneys will be in danger of being butchered by the King of Dahomey; others will be in peril from war, from false brethren, from pestilence and famine, from excess of cold and heat; others will be bowed down with sorrow and need comfort; some beset with temptation, and need help and guidance; while each and all ever, ever need the power of God's Spirit, and the showers of blessing which are promised in answer to prayer.

Then many of us have friends in different parts of the Mission field, and of course we should pay them a special visit when the day came in which we were to remember their station; and it would be very sweet to think that so many dear children were paying visits to the different Mission stations on the same day.

Shall we try? God is sure to answer prayer if it is offered in the name of Jesus, and for things touching his kingdom. He says in his word, "Ask of me, and I will give thee the heathen for thine inheritance, and the uttermost ends of the earth for thy possession."

For Him shall endless prayer be made,
And praises throng to crown his head;
His name, like sweet perfume shall rise,
With every morning sacrifice

WE LOVE

HIM

BECAUSE

HE

FIRST LOVED

US.

1 JOHN, iv. 19.

MISSIONARIES GOING TO FIJI.

MANY years ago a ship was sailing in the South Seas near the Fiji islands. Most of you know that the people who live in these islands were cannibals—that is, man-eaters: they eat one another, they eat their enemies whom they took in battle, and they eat white men when they could catch them.

Captains of ships sailing near those islands were afraid of these cannibals, and not without reason, for the sailors in many ships had been killed and eaten by them. The captain of the ship you see in the picture is taking care they shall not come on board his ship. He has some netting put up

round the sides of his ship: these are called boarding-nets, and they are fixed up to prevent anybody getting on the deck. The men on board are standing with fixed bayonets ready to stick into any of these savages if they tried to climb over the boarding-nets.

But why was the captain sailing there? Why did he go so near the islands that the Fijians could harm him?

The reason was, that he had got two Missionaries on board, who were going to these cannibals to preach the Gospel to them, and try to persuade them to leave off their horrible sins: these Missionaries had their wives with them. "What!" you say, "women go to these savage islands, where even armed men are afraid to go!" It was even so: these Christian women, the bravest of the brave, went with their husbands, and shared their dangers, that they might tell the wretched Fijian women about the love of Christ. It was Christ who put the desire to go into their hearts, and they knew He would go with them; they knew He *could* preserve them from all danger, and they believed He *would*.

Look at them as they are going into the Fiji canoe: calm and fearless, they put themselves into the power of the natives, who are ready to receive them. And did these savages murder and eat them? I think I hear some of you ask. No, they did not. God *did* take care of them. He blessed them, and He blessed their work; and thousands of Christian Fijians are now living to bless the Lord for sending those brave Missionaries and their wives to them, to lead them to the Lamb of God who taketh away the sins of even the cannibal Fijians.

SAYINGS AND DOINGS AMONG THE NAMACQUAS IN SOUTH AFRICA.

Mr. Priestley is a Missionary in South Africa: he thinks that the young friends who read the "Juvenile Offering" would like to hear something about the people he is living with, so he has written down little things that happened from day to day, and the talk he has had with the people. You will see how greedy and covetous some of the people are, and how many trials of faith and patience the Missionary has.

A rich native comes to Mr. Priestley with a contribution to the Mission.

Missionary enters the donation on the list. He then says that he is surprised to see so able a man bring a *sheep* as his contribution for the year. He reads out the names of those who have given oxen or cows many of whom are poorer than he.

Man says it was his intention to give a *beast*, but his cattle post is so far off that he thinks Mijnherr cannot wait so long a time as would be necessary to fetch it.

Missionary—"But you have long known that the Missionary meeting would be held this month. You have had *all the year* to prepare."

Man, being ashamed of his contribution, takes his sheep home again, and promises to give an ox.

A BELL IS WANTED FOR THE MISSION.

Missionary sends for the old ex-Chief, who is a blind man. He comes, accompanied by his guide, who is also an *interpreter*.

Missionary tells him that he wishes to have a larger church bell procured for the station, the present one being too small for all the people to hear, and asks if he is willing to contribute a couple of oxen with which to purchase the same, telling him he thinks it would be a nice present to the people of his tribe before he dies.

Ex-Chief agrees to the proposal, promises the oxen, and goes away.

A few days after, he comes with his guide to greet, as he is going away.

Missionary asks, what about the oxen he promised for the bell?

Ex-Chief.—"I will think about it."

Miss.—"But shall I depend on you, or ask some other person to give them? Besides, I want to accomplish the thing *immediately:* there is now an opportunity for having the bell brought from Cape Town."

Ex-Chief asks for a making of *tea* to drink before he leaves, and says that while he is drinking the tea he will turn the matter over in his mind.

Missionary refuses the tea, and says, "You know it is not our custom to give to persons who beg."

Ex-Chief takes his hat, and, walking away, says, "Then I shall not give the oxen. I am too poor to do so."

Miss.—"Very well."

As he goes away he is overheard to say, "I don't know how it was I was so foolish as to promise the oxen."

(*To be continued.*)

A JUBILEE MEETING IN THE CITY OF MYSORE.

Some of my young readers may have attended a Jubilee Meeting of the Wesleyan Missionary Society in this country, and very much, I dare say, you enjoyed it. You were told how that, fifty years ago, this Society was begun, and many other interesting particulars.

But this Jubilee of ours is a world-wide festival: in India, Africa, and Australia the Jubilee Hymn is sung, and thanksgiving and praise offered up by people of many languages and colour.

I will tell you how the Missionaries and the Christians of the city of Mysore kept their Jubilee Meeting. Mrs. Hutcheon, the Missionary's wife, writes the account.

She says, "I must turn to a brighter scene now, and tell you how we, in this fettered, caste-bound land, hailed the soul-stirring blast of the Jubilee trumpet.

We celebrated the memorable 6th of October, both publicly and privately, with grateful hearts, and felt throughout the day an unwonted joy; but it was in the evening that all the emotions of our hearts were called into liveliest exercise.

We invited all our native Christians to come and rejoice with us; and I had provided some of the good things of this life, such as coffee, cake, &c., to which some fifty sat down. Then followed the baptism of a young convert, prayer, and hearty Jubilee addresses, varied by singing, which altogether would not have disgraced a Leeds meeting, though in a strange tongue. It was no common joy to look around on so many fine youths, as well as men whose hoary hairs reminded us that, ere long, they would be celebrating a higher Jubilee in nobler and more exalted strains, and to feel that they were the living fruits of the faith, zeal, and love, that day so forcibly called to mind. Surely the next fifty years will witness results of which these are but foretastes."

THE
WESLEYAN JUVENILE OFFERING.

AN APPEAL TO THE CHILDREN OF GREAT BRITAIN ON BEHALF OF THE CHILDREN OF INDIA.

THERE is a Society called the *Christian Vernacular Education Society for India.* It has, you see, a rather long name, and there is one word which, perhaps, you have not seen before; I mean the word *vernacular.* It means native language. The Society's object is to give the children of India a Christian education in their own native languages.

The kind friends who support this Society are anxious that the children in England should do what they can to help the children in India, and you will, I am sure, like to read, what they say about them.

"India contains a large number of children. Indeed, there are as many children in that land as there are men, women, and children in the British isles. These young people have none of the advantages you enjoy in this happy Christian land. You have kind and good teachers, who instruct you in what is useful to know while passing through this world, and point out the way to a happier one to come. And you have good and useful books, but very few of the children have either Christian teachers or books. Not *one hundred thousand* of them are under Christian instruction. This is a small number out of *thirty millions*.

"Perhaps you ask, are they left to grow up in total ignorance? Most of the girls are. They are not allowed to learn any thing. Only the boys go to school. In the picture in the front page you see two Hindu boys in Southern India on their way to school. Some of the schools are kept under a tree, and some in the verandah, which is a shaded place in front of the house.

"In these schools they do not learn much, and in most of them the children have neither books, nor maps, nor slates. In some the boys use books made of the leaves of the palm-tree, which they carry to school between two boards, in the way represented in the engraving. All they learn is a little reading, writing, and arithmetic; but even these things, so necessary for every one to know, they do not learn properly. Worse than all, they are taught to worship idols!

"Many of the lessons given them are very bad, as the following anecdote will show:—A Missionary asked a respectable native to write out some of the lessons he used to learn when a boy. He began to do so, but could not go on. He asked the Missionary to excuse him doing the rest, because the lessons he had learnt were so wicked and vile. He said he was quite ashamed of them, and wished he could wash them all away from his memory.

"At the present time nearly *thirty millions* of children in India are being taught by heathen teachers. Never do they hear of the true and living God, or of the Saviour Jesus Christ, or of the happy home in glory which He has prepared for all who love Him. Dear young friends, will you help to give them Christian teachers and books?"

SAYINGS AND DOINGS OF THE NAMACQUAS IN SOUTH AFRICA.

The richest man in the land, says Mr. Priestley, who is Missionary to these Namacquas, comes to ask if the Missionary has a pair of *spectacles* he can spare, as he wants to read, but his sight is too short.

Missionary.—"I have a pair of *green* spectacles as eye-preservers, but I have none to sell."

Man.—"Can I see what you have?"

Missionary.—"Yes, I can let you see them, but they are not for sale." (Two pairs are found and shown.)

Man.—"But cannot Mijnheer part with *one* pair, for I am in great need?"

Missionary.—"Well, as I see I have *two* pairs, I will make you a *present* of *one.*"

Man.—"Thank you, but cannot I get the other also for my wife?"

Missionary.—"Well, if you wish to have them, in order to help you to *read*, I will try to spare them;

I can get another pair, perhaps. You shall have the *second* pair for the same price I paid in Cape Town."

Man.—"How much did you pay?"

(The amount is named.)

Man.—The price is too high for me."

Missionary.—"Well, that is what I gave for them: if it is too high for you don't take them."

Man.—"I will give you *a sheep* for them."

Missionary.—"No; I must have *cash*, with which to buy myself another pair."

Man.—"I have not cash, so I will leave them."

Missionary.—"Very well."

(Next morning he comes again, bringing his wife also. They want the spectacles, though they are dear: the wife cannot do without them.)

Missionary.—"Well, I said you can have them for the price I gave. Bring the money, and then you shall have them."

(The money is brought.)

Missionary.—"But you said last night you had no money, and now I see the money comes. How is that?"

Man.—"My meaning was, I did not wish to give cash for the spectacles; I would rather give a sheep."

Missionary.—"But you spoke an untruth."

Man.—"Yes; I spoke wrong last night. Mijnheer must *forgive* me."

Missionary.—"It is a sin against *God*, and you must seek forgiveness of Him, or He will call you to account for this untruth."

THE HORSEBREAKER.

A man having been engaged to train two or three young horses for the Society, is asked what remuneration he will expect for the trouble.

Man.—"The other Missionaries generally gave me a pair of trousers.

Missionary.—"Well, I am willing to give you what the other Missionaries gave you."

(An arrangement is made, that for each horse he shall have a pair of trousers, or any thing that is of the same value, and the man is satisfied.)

The first horse being trained, he comes to ask for payment.

Missionary.—"What shall I give you this time, a pair of trousers, or some other article?"

Man.—"I want *a saddle.*

Missionary.—"But a saddle is a very dear article, and I agreed to give you a pair of trousers, or what was of equal value."

Man.—"But I understood that I was to have any thing that I needed at the time."

Missionary. — "I never said so. If *that* were the arrangement, it might happen that you wanted a wagon, and would ask *that.* I will give you according to the agreement. Don't you know there is a great deal of difference in the value of a saddle and a pair of trousers? In this country you must give two large oxen if you would purchase a saddle."

Man.—"But is the value of a saddle more than my trouble in learning a horse?"

Missionary.—"I say nothing about your trouble in learning the horse; what I will give you is just what other persons get for the same work, and what *you* said you got from the other Missionaries."

(The man is greatly dissatisfied that he cannot get a saddle, and talks a good deal about it, speaking very improper language. At last he takes a jacket, and goes away, resolving never to help the Missionary again.)

同治二年

聖經擇要詳論

羊城增沙惠師禮堂鐫

MR. WESLEY'S SERMONS IN CHINESE.

MR. PIERCEY, Missionary in China, has been translating some of Mr. Wesley's Sermons into the Chinese language. I thought you would like to see the title-page of this book of sermons, and so it is copied on the other page, and you may know what it is like.

The title-page of a book is the first page which tells you what the book is about. In a Chinese book the letters or characters are put in lines from the top of the page to the bottom, instead of being put across the page, as in an English book. So you begin reading the large characters in the middle of the page, and read down from top to bottom.

The meaning in English is this, "SELECT DISCOURSES ON IMPORTANT PASSAGES OF HOLY SCRIPTURES." The meaning of the smaller characters on the right side of the page is, "The second year of Tung chi." Tung chi is the name of the Chinese Emperor, and it means that the book was printed in the second year of his reign. The characters on the left side are, "Printed at the Wesleyan Chapel, Sand Street, in the city of Rams." Rams is the poetical name for Canton.

The five sermons which Mr. Piercey has translated are printed in the same small characters as at the side.

It is a good thing to have Wesley's Sermons printed in Chinese, at a Wesleyan Chapel in China. If Mr. Wesley could have foreseen this, how his heart would have rejoiced to think, that to the ends of the world the news of salvation was taken, and that the very sermons which he was preaching to the sinners in England, calling them to turn from their sins to God, would be preached to the sinners in China, and that the Chinese would listen to them, and, forsaking their idols, would serve the living and true God.

A STORY FROM HUDSON'S BAY.

SAVED BY HIS TEETH.

EXTRACT of a Letter from the Rev. Charles Stringfellow, dated Norway House, Rossville, 25th December, 1863:—

"One of our leaders (Henry Budd) had a providential escape from drowning this winter. He is a servant of the Hudson's Bay Company, and in the fall and early winter is employed in fishing. After the setting fast of the water, the fishing nets are put under the ice. The Indians do not always wait till it is strong, but cross it when it is weak. They creep along on their hands and knees, or they walk with a pole six or eight feet long in their hand, sounding the ice every few steps. Henry thought the ice strong enough, yoked his dogs, sat on his sled, and drove to the holes where he had put in his nets. He drove briskly across the ice until he came to where the current is strong under it—here he found the ice to bend, and in a few seconds more, dogs, sled and driver were in the lake—had gone through the ice. His companion, Edward Papanakiss was behind with sled and dogs, but slid off his sled and allowed the dogs to go on alone, and escaped. Edward would have gone to Henry, but on no account would he permit him. He knew it would be death to both if Edward came near. For himself he was ready to depart, knowing that death is gain to the Christian. Henry clave to the edge of the ice — it gave way frequently — he swam and took hold again and again. His fingers were benumbed with cold, and so was his body—the dogs were drawing him down like a dead weight, as they were entangled and could not rise. His companion ran for a rope, and was an hour and a half in bringing it, such was the distance; mean time Henry was still clinging, though he was resigned to death. At last the rope was thrown, but alas! it was too late, his limbs were stiff and fingers frozen. God helped him. The rope was once more thrown, it was caught in his teeth, and by his teeth he was drawn out of the water, nearly frozen. With proper remedies and care he has come round again, and is now well, excepting the ends of his fingers, which are still numb."

REAPING IN JOY—JUBILEE MEETING IN FIJI.

The sound of the Jubilee trumpet has reached us all the way from Fiji. Mr. Calvert has held a Jubilee Meeting in Fiji, where, twenty years ago, he landed amidst savage cannibals. How little did he think then that there would be so many thousand Christian Fijians celebrating with us this our Missionary Jubilee! We adore and wonder at the grace and mercy shewn by our loving Saviour to cannibal Fiji.

JUBILEE MEETING.

The day fixed for the Meeting was the day twenty-five years when Mr. Calvert first landed in Fiji. The king was going to build a Jubilee church, and Mr. Calvert was to plant the first post. In England we build with bricks, stone, and mortar, and the foundation-stone is laid with a trowel, generally a silver one; but in Fiji the chapel was to be built with wood, and Mr. Calvert was to plant a post. A grand mallet was made for the occasion instead of a trowel: it was of wood, inlaid with whale's tooth and pearl shell: I suppose the people made it as handsome as they could.

Early in the morning people arrived from all the outer towns, bringing cooked food, which the king shared out, sending a goodly portion to the Mission-house, which was divided among the carpenters, native assistant Missionaries, students, and both the Mission families.

At eleven they assembled in the chapel. Matthias, the teacher in the king's town, who was an active, useful lad to Mr. Calvert in his first voyage twenty-four years ago, offered an earnest prayer. After a short address in a rejoicing strain, by Mr. Tait, he called up Zaccheus, a Christian Fijian, to read a letter from the king and people to Mr. and Mrs. Calvert.

This address was to tell them how thankful they were to God that Mr. Calvert had come to them, and how different many parts of Fiji were now they have the holy Scriptures, and know and love the true God.

After the address was read, Mr. Calvert made a speech to the people; then he baptized twelve grown-up people and two children: after that three of the chiefs delivered addresses.

THE NEW CHURCH.

They then adjourned to the site of the new church, which was marked out. It is to be an octagonal building, sixty-two feet across, with a verandah all round, projecting six feet and a half, making the extreme width seventy-five feet. The estimated cost is twenty-six tuns of cocoa-nut oil, worth from 20*l.* to 22*l.* on the spot, and 34*l.* in Sydney.

I wish we could see this new Jubilee church: perhaps, when it is finished, some one will send us a picture of it.

PLANTING THE FIRST POST.

A hymn was sung, composed for the occasion by Mr. Tait, who then presented Mr. Calvert, on behalf of the Building Committee, with a wooden mallet, inlaid with whale's tooth and pearl-shell, and an iron-wood digging stick, wherewith he set the first post, following the usual form of laying a foundation-stone at home. Afterwards he delivered a short address to the surrounding multitude, encouraging them in the great work which they had cheerfully and nobly undertaken. The children of Tumbou and other towns then chanted a song, which they had got up to welcome the visit of Mr. and Mrs. Calvert.

TAKE CARE OF THE LAMBS.

A GENTLEMAN was walking over his farm with a friend, exhibiting his crops, herds of cattle, and flocks of sheep, with all of which his friend was highly pleased, but with nothing so much as his splendid sheep. He had seen the same breed frequently before, but had never seen such noble specimens; and with great earnestness he asked how he had succeeded in rearing such flocks. His simple answer was, "I take care of my lambs, sir." Here was all the secret—he took care of his lambs!

Reader—father, mother, teacher—need we make the application?

I,

EVEN I,

AM THE LORD;

AND BESIDE

ME

THERE IS NO

SAVIOUR.

ISAIAH xliii. 11.

Tune sung to Kafir Evening Hymn.

ANGELUS. Rev. A. Brigg.

Savuka sipilile,
  Kwa ngobubele bayo ;
Kaloku sekuhlwile,
  Sisenenklalo ngayo.
Samkel' ukutya kwetu,
Kwa nesivato setu,
Sanikw' indhlela yetu,
  Ngalo ufefe lwayo.

Solala ngokwonwaba,
  Ngobubusuku bonke ;
Asikwoyika 'ntshaba,
  In-kos' ipezu kwonko ;
Yobona xa silele,
Yoman' isikangele,
Yowenza ngobubele,
  Kwa ngamaxesha onke.

SUCKING HONEY FROM A ROCK.

In Deut. xxxii. 13, it is said of the Israelites in the wilderness, that God made them to *suck honey out of the rock.*

In Africa the bees deposit their honey on the trunks of trees and on rocks. Trees in some countries being scarce, the honey in most parts is found upon the front of rocks or cliffs, plastered on the outside, having a covering of wax to protect it from intruders. This outside coating, after a short exposure to the weather, assumes nearly the same colour as the rock, which, at a little distance, cannot easily be distinguished from the rock; so that a person making an incision with a knife, and putting his mouth to it to suck it, were a person a little way off to notice some of the honey dropping from his chin, would believe that he saw a man sucking honey from a rock; so the Scripture method of expressing it is very beautiful.

There is an allusion to the same thing, Isaiah lxxxi. 16: " He should have fed them also with the finest of the wheat, and with honey out of the rock should I have satisfied thee."

I remember seeing in a boor's house in the Cape Colony, the greater part of the gable at the end of his garret plastered over with honey by the bees. When the boor required a portion of honey for his table, he cut away, perhaps, a square foot of the hive, when the bees immediately set to work to fill up with fresh honey the vacuum he had made. In this way he said, he kept them always at work.

REV. JOHN CAMPBELL.

THE

WESLEYAN JUVENILE OFFERING.

OLD DAVID AND HIS LITTLE INDIAN SCHOLARS.

OLD DAVID is teacher in the Madras girls' school: he has taught in the school for fourteen years, and how pleasant it looks to be sitting in the shade of the tree hearing the children say their alphabet, or teaching them to write the letters in the sand.

The bigger girls stay in the schoolroom, and I dare say you would like to hear what they learn. Miss Clayton, their teacher, says, "The school opens at half-past nine in the morning, with singing a hymn in Tamil; then they have prayers in Tamil. There are fifty-eight children in the school. These Indian girls learn geography, arithmetic, and Scripture history: many of them learn to read and speak English. Very clever some of these children are: they crochet beautifully, and do plain work very well.

But what is best of all, these children learn to know and love Jesus, instead of hearing the wicked, stupid stories of heathen gods. Their kind teacher tells them about the blessed Saviour who loves little children so much, and who said, "Suffer the little children to come to me, and forbid them not." And some of these dear children do go to Him, and one of them He has taken to be with Him in heaven. Three days before she died, she said, "Jesus makes me quite happy." Her schoolfellows were the mourners at her grave, and some of them wish to follow her to heaven, and are seeking to know and love Jesus. One evening the governess was sitting in the schoolroom, after school was over, and she heard low murmuring sounds from different parts of the room, and, on looking round, saw it was the children who were engaged in prayer. The little ones go to the elder ones, and ask them to talk to them about Jesus.

Does it not make your hearts glad to hear this good news from a heathen land? But, dear children, you who live in this Christian land, do you love to hear about your blessed Saviour as these Hindoo scholars do? They are surrounded by idolatry and wicked superstitions; but with all their hearts they try to please God, and to become lambs of Christ's flock.

Are you as earnest and prayerful? If not, pray that God may give you his Holy Spirit to incline your heart to love Him. How great will be your condemnation if these children of a heathen land enter into heaven and you are shut out!

ALMOST THERE.

"I AM almost there!"
Said a dying child,
As she upward looked
And sweetly smiled;
"The happy homes
Of the blest I see,
And an angel band
Awaiting me.

"I am almost there!
But do not weep;
In a Saviour's arms
It is sweet to sleep."
And she closed her eyes,
And gently placed
Her folded hands
Across her breast.

"I am almost there!
Sweet Jesus, now,"
And the damps of death
O'erspread her brow,
And her brightening features
Almost smiled,
As we wept beside
The dying child.

KAFIR SUPERSTITIONS.

Mr. Briggs, who is a Missionary among the Kaffirs, has sent you some accounts of the native superstitions popularly believed by their various tribes. He says they will show the young people of England how dark and ignorant are the poor heathen, to whom the Missionaries have come to lead them to Jesus.

BELIEF IN SPIRITS

The Kafirs and Fingoes have a singular belief in a power residing in streams and rivers. To give it a definite form, I will call it *the spirit of the waters.* They believe that this spirit has the power of *calling* people. A Kafir, in his house, or his field, or perhaps when in conversation with others, all at once imagines himself "*called by the river.*" He immediately rushes down to the water, and, according to the impression he there receives, either casts himself into the stream, or kills an ox, or a goat on the bank, and throws all the flesh into the water. A case occurred not very long ago, at one of the stations in British Kaffraria. A Kafir girl was seen rushing impetuously to the river. Some people tried to detain her, but she would not be hindered, declaring that "the river had called her." She was never heard of afterwards.

They believe further that the *spirit of the waters* has the power of inflicting diseases upon those who refuse to obey the call.

Once when I was travelling with my interpreter, near Mount Coke, he entered into conversation with a boy whose face was much disfigured by an eruption. He said to the boy, "What is the matter with your face?" "Oh! it's the river!" was the reply. "What do you mean? How can the river make your face so?" "Are you such a fool as not to know about the spirit of the river?" said the boy, "Once that river was *very strong:* people could not play with it then. But now so much soap is put into it by the Christians washing their clothes there, that it is not so strong as it was; but you see in my face what it can do!"

THE CHILD'S GOSPEL.

A VERY little girl had been early taken to church, and taught to behave reverently there. She was told that public worship had been appointed by God, and that she must attend seriously to its several parts, until she should be old enough to comprehend them. So she would fix her eyes attentively on the preacher, and listen to all he said, though able to understand but little.

But once a smile of joy was observed to pass over her expressive face. Her eye grew bright, and her red lips parted as if to speak. She had been repaid for her docile listening. In the midst of his discourse, the minister repeated the Saviour's invitation, "Suffer little children to come unto me, and forbid them not."

Hastening home to her mother, who had been detained by indisposition from the public services of the Sabbath, she threw her arms around her neck, exclaiming with great animation, "Oh, mamma, dear mamma, I have heard to-day *the child's gospel.*"

THIS IS

HIS COMMANDMENT,

THAT WE SHOULD

LOVE ONE ANOTHER

AS HE GAVE

US

COMMANDMENT.

TRANSLATION OF KAFFIR EVENING HYMN.*

We still on earth are living;
We still all good receiving;
From evil to deliver,
God's own right hand has ever
Been our sure guard, confessing,
We offer thanks and blessing;
Let all with reverence lowly,
Adore the Lord most holy.

With early morn awaking
In health; all good partaking,
We passed the day; till even
Darkens the clouds of heaven.
The Lord of life still reigning,
By food our life sustaining,
With raiment too has clad us,
And by his light has led us.

To sleep our souls composing,
Throughout the night reposing,
We rest in peace, not fearing
The foe, however daring.
The eye of God beholding,
The arm of God enfolding,
From Him what can us sever?
He will forsake us never!

* Mr. Briggs sent the Kaffir Hymn, which, with the music, you had in the last month's "Juvenile Offering." This English translation can be sung to the same tune.—See page 110.

GIBRALTAR.

HAVE you a brother or a cousin in the army, or any friend a soldier? You know he may be sent out of England to foreign countries whenever the Government may think fit. Many soldiers are sent to Gibraltar to be ready for service in the Mediterranean or in North Africa. Some soldiers who were in Gibraltar sixty years ago met together to read the Bible and to pray one with another. They had a room to meet in, which became too small when the Committee sent a Missionary to preach to them. They got a larger room, and then a larger, until at last they built the neat chapel you see in the picture. It is a soldiers' chapel, and is filled every Sunday with men, in their red coats, and their wives and children. What a comfort that the Methodist soldiers in Gibraltar are well cared for.

But there are many people in Gibraltar besides soldiers. There are many Spaniards and many Jews. The Missionaries have preached to the Spaniards in the Spanish language, and have talked to the Jews in Hebrew and in Arabic. They have given Bibles to the Roman Catholics and Testaments to the Jews. Several Jews have become Christians. One of them is now a clergyman in London, and one is a Missionary to the Jews. The chapel in Gibraltar has been a great blessing, and, we hope, will continue to be so.

WESLEYAN MISSIONARY.

Mr. Alton is the Missionary now in Gibraltar: he can preach in Spanish as well as in English. Mr. Alton went to Spain to preach to the Spaniards, but the priests would not let him stay.

There is a bad religion in Spain—the Roman Catholic. The priests do not read the Bible much, nor do they advise the people to read it, though the Bible is the book which can make us wise, and save our souls; so they tried by all means in their power to get Mr. Alton sent away, and at last they succeeded. If he had remained he would have been sent to prison.

There was a good man who wished to give Bibles and Testaments to the Spaniards, so he hired a donkey, and loaded it with a bag of books. As he went along, a young woman passed, leading a little boy by the hand. She stopped him, and said, "Uncle, what have you got on your ass?"

Why did she call him uncle? It is a name that people in Spain often give to strangers, when they wish to speak civilly. The young woman said, "Have you got soap on your ass?"

The stranger told the young woman that he sold good books, and he showed her a Testament. She began to read out loud, and at last cried out, "What beautiful, what charming reading!" Then she inquired the price of the book. Though it was very cheap, she said she had not money enough to buy it; so she put it down, and went away. But soon the little boy came running back, shouting out, "Stop, uncle! the book! the book!" The little fellow had got the money for it in his hand, but it was all in copper, not in silver.

A few of the priests, when they saw the good man's Bibles, praised them, and bought some; but most of the priests were angry, and spoke against the holy books. Poor people bought them. Many of them had never seen a Testament before. Sometimes a poor man would sit under the shade of a great tree, while his neighbours would gather round and listen attentively to the history of the Lord Jesus. You have heard that history. You have a Bible or a Testament of your own. Do you love it?

THE PRISON.

The gentleman who sold Bibles in Spain was shut up for three weeks in a prison in Madrid. It was a horrible place. In the day the prisoners walked about in large courts, but at night they were all locked up in dark dungeons. There were no beds, but only horse-cloths spread on the floor. The darkest and dirtiest of all the dungeons was one in which the little thieves were locked up, poor boys who had scarcely a rag to cover them.

THE COTTAGES.

In some parts of Spain there are rows of neat white cottages, with red-tiled roofs. But when the door of a cottage is open, you see at the end of the narrow passage an altar to the Virgin Mary, with little pictures placed above it. In Spain the Virgin Mary is worshipped more than God. How much grieved the blessed Mary would be could she hear the prayers and praises that are offered up to her. She would say, "Go to, my son; He saved me, and He is able to save you."

INVITATION TO THE HEATHEN CHILD.

LITTLE wandering lamb,
  Whither stray?
Jesus calls—"I am
  The truth, the way."

Oh turn and seek his fold,
  Enter in:
All cannot be told,
  You shall win.

Children, he delights
  To receive:
You, he now invites:
  Oh! Believe!

Though you never knew
  Ev'n his name,
Yet to die for you
  To earth he came.

Yes, for you he here
  Was crucified:
Come and drop a tear
  That He died.

If you seek his love,
 You shall know
Blessing far above
 All earth can show.

Listen! Hear him call:
 Say, "Yes, I flee
From sin, from evil, all,
 Saviour, to thee."

There rest and never stray,
 Thy home is there:
Oh, seek Him day by day,
 In praise and prayer.

Within his fold on earth,
 Watch'd by his eye,
Till born in better birth
 When thou shalt die.

Led to his own right hand,
 In robes of light,
Thou shalt hereafter stand,
 An angel bright.

Then little wandering lamb,
 Whither stray?
Jesus calls—"I am
 The truth, the way.

JAMES EDMESTON.

THE NAMACQUA WHO WISHED TO SERVE GOD.

I HAVE told you of some of the discouragements that Mr. Priestley has among the Namacquas: now I will tell you of some things that he has to cheer him. He finds that all his labour is not in vain.

Hearing an unusual noise in our kitchen one Sunday evening, while at tea, I left the sitting-room to see what it was.

One of the station-men (Adam Kaffer) was in earnest conversation with our servant-boy.

Missionary.—"What is the matter?"

(After some little hesitation,)

The Man began. "I am just telling Samson that I feel myself to be *a great sinner*, and unworthy to walk upon the ground."

Missionary.—"I am glad to hear you have been brought to see that. The last time I spoke with you about your soul you told me these matters did not trouble your head."

Man.—"The sermons of to-day have made me feel as I never felt before."

Missionary.—"It is a matter of thankfulness that you have been brought to see your need of a Saviour. What is then your determination?"

Man.—"I will begin to serve God this very night."

Missionary.—That is a good resolution; I will pray for you, and will be glad to help you in any way I possibly can."

YOUTHS SEEKING SALVATION.

After conducting family worship before leaving home on my monthly visit to Hoole's Fountain, our two servant boys made us acquainted with the fact that they had got a desire to serve the Lord. After speaking to them, and giving them suitable advice, I asked the *third* youth (Klein David Jager) present, a young man who was there for a few days helping us, and was to remain at home to care for the house, cattle, &c.), if *he* also had not a like desire?

Boy.—"I am not ready yet, but think I shall be soon."

Missionary.—"I hope that while we are away you will think about the matter, and be fully ready when we return."

On reaching home, I asked him what text the native preacher had taken on the Sabbath I was absent.

Boy.—"The man cutting the child in two!" (Solomon's decision in the case of the two women, though I suppose this must have been the *lesson* read.

Afterwards I asked him if he were yet ready to serve God.

Boy.—"Yes, I am ready now."

Missionary.—"What has brought you to decision?"

Boy.—"The text about cutting the child in two!"

Having asked two or three of the principal men (members of society) to drink tea one afternoon, that we might hear something as to the means by which they were brought to God, their present religious experience, &c., the conversation turned on the prospect of the Mission.

One (Jan Ortman) said, "I don't know whether the word of God will stay in this land. I fear it will go away." Then, turning to another, he asked, "Supposing you had cultivated a garden for many years, and it brought nothing forth, would you continue to cultivate that garden?"

He then remarked, "Some people in this land say they can do without the word, and without a Missionary. But I don't say so. It is true God is *everywhere*, and so it is true WOOD is everywhere; but if there is no FIRE how shall the wood burn?

TREADING ON SERPENTS AND SCORPIONS.

JESUS said unto his disciples, before sending them forth to preach the Gospel all over the world, "Behold, I give you power *to tread on serpents and scorpions*, and over all the power of the enemy; and nothing shall by any means hurt you."—*Luke* x. 9.

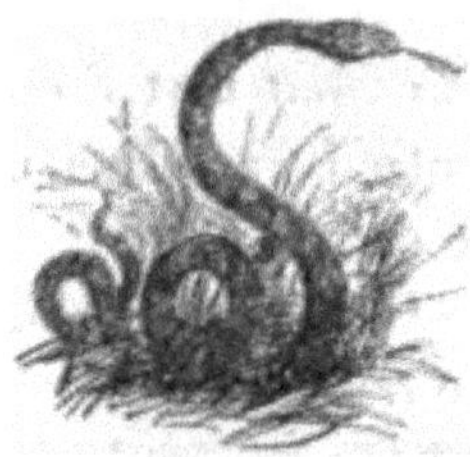

Jesus first sent out upon a preaching tour twelve disciples, then seventy. On their return they expressed their astonishment at the power which attended the use they made of the name of Jesus, especially the flight of devils from those possessed by them at the very mention of this name. On this, and seemingly in view of the long journey over the world which lay before them, Jesus gave unto them the above address.

Serpents generally are timid, and run from men. The chief danger from serpents in the day-time arises from *treading* on them among grass, which conceals them from the notice of the pedestrian, or in the night time on roads; in both which cases they bite directly.

A scorpion is but a small animal, only a few inches long, but extremely poisonous. Little danger can arise from treading on them, to a person wearing boots or shoes; but in eastern countries, where sandals are worn which only cover the soles of the feet, it must frequently have been mortal to tread on the scorpion also, especially among grass.—REV. J. CAMPBELL.

THE

WESLEYAN JUVENILE OFFERING.

DEATH OF THE NATIVE MINISTER OF ABBEOKUTA.

OUR young readers will be sorry to hear of the death of the Rev. Edward Bickersteth, the native minister at Abbeokuta. He died of dysentery after a few days' illness, and has left a widow and five children to mourn his loss.

He was an Egba, born in Kesi, one of the town

destroyed by war. Abbeokuta contains something like 130 remnants of towns which have been swept away by the slave wars. Such of the people as were spared took shelter together, and built the town called Abbeokuta, or "Under the stone," it being built round the great rock called Olumo.

Mr. Bickersteth was captured at the time Kesi was destroyed, which will be about forty years ago. He was sold by the cruel warriors to the Portuguese slave-dealers, who placed him, in company with many other unfortunates, on board a ship, intending to sell him at the Brazils or Cuba; but while the slaver was crossing the Atlantic, she was seen, chased, and taken as a prize, and very soon, with her living freight, brought to Sierra Leone, where all the captives were made free. The children, among whom was our departed friend, were put to school, and he received the name of Edward Bickersteth. He soon learned to read and write the English language, then took a situation as clerk in one of the Government offices, from whence he went to teach in one of the Wesleyan schools. While in the employment of our Society he was brought to know his danger as a sinner. He repented, and, trusting in Jesus Christ, was pardoned and made happy.

Some years afterwards, a teacher was wanted for Abbeokuta. The Rev. Henry Badger was then Superintendent at Sierra Leone. He thought Edward Biskersteth was the right man, and asked him to go; so, in company with his wife, he set sail for Badagry, and from thence up the country to the place where he finished his labours; where, in company with Mr. Morgue, he began to preach. The Lord blessed their labours, and a little society was soon formed. Mr. Morgue, after some time, was removed to another station, so Mr. Bickersteth was left in charge. He became an eloquent and useful preacher in the language, and many souls will thank God in heaven that Edward Bickersteth returned to his native land as a preacher of the Gospel.

But he is gone, and is at rest. Will you not pray to God to comfort the bereaved widow, and to provide for the fatherless children? And also that some one may be raised up to take his place?

Mr. Sykes, who went out to succeed Mr. Champness, is now alone. This is very trying, as there is much to be done, and, especially, as there is now another chapel, three miles from the old one, which needs attention. It is to be hoped that where the new chapel is there will be another station some day. The new chapel was built in part by money given to Mr. Bickersteth when he was on a visit to his old friends in Sierra Leone. The money subscribed was not enough, however, and a debt of *27l.* was left upon it; but when Mr. Champness returned to England, some of the friends in the circuit where he resided before going to Africa determined to pay off the debt. At Lady-barn, a small school chapel in the Manchester fifth circuit, the ladies began to work and beg, until they had sufficient materials for a Missionary tree, which was exhibited in the new school-room at Rusholme; and though the night was wet and stormy, the money needed was raised, and handed over to Mr. Champness. The Bible used in the new chapel was given by the children of St. George's Sunday-school, and the Hymn-book by the school at Rusholme. The pulpit cushion was also a present, given by friends at Newton Heath.

Are there not other places which have sent out men as Missionaries who might help the cause, as these kind friends have done? Has your circuit sent out a preacher to the heathen? Then ask yourselves the question, What can we do to cheer him in his toil? Has he a chapel or school that wants help? Then let us show him that, though absent, he is not forgotten.

You cannot tell how much you would cheer the labourer in his work, if you would do as the friends at Lady-barn have done for Abbeokuta.

THOMAS CHAMPNESS.

HELP ONE ANOTHER.

A TRAVELLER, who was crossing the Alps, was overtaken by a snow-storm at the top of a high mountain. The cold became intense. The air was thick with sleet, and the piercing wind seemed to penetrate his bones. Still the traveller, for a time, struggled on. But at last his limbs were benumbed, a heavy drowsiness began to creep over him, his feet almost refused to move, and he lay down on the snow to give way to that fatal sleep which is the last stage of extreme cold, and from which he would certainly never have waked again in this world.

Just at that moment he saw another poor traveller coming along the road. The unhappy man seemed to be, if possible, even in a worse condition than himself, for he, too, could scarcely move; all his powers were frozen, and he appeared to be just on the point to die.

When he saw this poor man, the traveller who was just going to lie down to sleep made a great effort. He roused himself up, and crawled, for he was scarcely able to walk, to his dying fellow-traveller.

He took his hands into his own, and tried to warm them. He chafed his temples; he rubbed his feet; he applied friction to his body. And all the time he spoke cheering words into his ear, and tried to comfort him.

As he did this the dying man began to revive, his powers were restored, and he felt able to go forward. But this was not all, for his kind benefactor, too, was recovered by the efforts which he had made to save his friend. The exertion of rubbing made the blood circulate again in his own body. He grew warm by trying to warm the other. His drowsiness went off; he no longer wished to sleep; his limbs returned again to their proper force; and the travellers went on their way together happy, and congratulating one another on their escape.

Soon the snow-storm passed away, the mountain was crossed, and they reached their homes in safety.

If, dear reader, you feel your heart cold toward God, and your soul almost ready to perish, try to do something which may help another soul to life and make his heart glad; and you will often find it the best way to warm and restore and gladden your own.

LETTER FROM AN INDIAN SCHOOL-GIRL TO MRS. CAMPBELL.

"*Bangalore, Feb.* 23*d*, 1864.

"My dear Mother,—I received your kind and welcome letter; I was so glad that I could not tell, and I have much pleasure in writing these few lines to you, hoping that you are well, and we are the same at present, thanks be to the Lord for his mercy towards us. I am sorry to say that our dear mother, Mrs. Rice, was very ill, but, by the care of God, she is a little better, blessed be the Lord God, who has been gracious to her.

Dear mother, I often think about England, and of the gardens, and of the mineral waters. I should be so glad if I was there, but I shall never come; but there is another place so happy on the other side of Jordan, in the sweet fields of Eden, where the tree of life is blooming. There is rest for the weary. Oh! I long to be there. I hope all of my companions may be there.

Dear mother, our school is filled with little children: there are twenty-eight girls, and I hope God will gather more children into it. On Sunday we have a Bible class, and we learn chapters and hymns, which is very interesting, and dear Mrs. Rice takes much pains to teach us. In your letter you told me that I must write to Hannie Thomas. I will try to write to her, and please tell her that I am not entirely educated in English, but part in English and part in Canarese, so that I cannot write English so clearly.

Dear mother, you told me to write about the Missionary meeting, but I do not know when that meeting is going to be held. I hope they will have it soon. Please give my best compliments to Mr. Campbell, and all the dear sisters in the school, and all the dear Christian friends send their love to you. Dear mother, I hope to meet you again. In the promised land, at Jesus' feet, a joyous band will praise Him in the promised land. If there are any mistakes in these few lines, please excuse them.

"I beg to remain,

"Your obedient and loving daughter,

"MARGARET."

THE PEARL.

A PERSIAN FABLE.

A LITTLE particle of rain,
 That from a passing cloud descended,
Was heard thus idly to complain—
 "My brief existence now is ended;
Outcast alike of earth and sky,
Useless to live—unknown to die."

It chanced to fall into the sea,
 And there an open shell received it;
And, after years how rich was he,
 Who from his prison-house released it!
That drop of rain had formed a gem
 Fit for a monarch's diadem.

A MISSIONARY RE-EMBARKING FOR ENGLAND.

This scene is well calculated to shew us the feelings entertained by the Africans towards their teachers. The Missionaries who labour at Sierra Leone are usually obliged to return to Europe at the end of every five or six years, to recruit their health, which rapidly gives way in that unhealthy part of Africa. These parting occasions are often quite affecting; for the natives are a warm-hearted people, and much attached to those who are "over them in the Lord." The Missionaries usually embark at the wharf, as represented in the pictures, and proceed in a small boat to the ship, not unfrequently accompanied by other boats, with some of the natives on board, bearing fruit and vegetables, &c., for the voyage.

We will give, as an instance of this, a Missionary's description of his departure from the colony:—

"As the time of separation drew on, it was moving to see, from the highest to the lowest, in and out of the church, many, with copious showers of tears and blessings on our heads, bringing their parting tokens of affection, in the shape of oranges, pine-apples, arrow root, &c. Could the friends of Missions have witnessed the scene presented at the wharf, they would have felt that the Africans are as affectionate and grateful for favours received as ever, and do highly value the labours of those who bring tidings of life and peace to them. The hour of embarkation was unknown, and scarcely the day; yet a large concourse of old and young had assembled to take a parting look. It was with difficulty we could get through them, and still more difficult to get their hands to release ours. The ship moving from the harbour was the signal for us to proceed on board, when such a burst of heartfelt grief rent the air as would have affected any heart. The scene reminded us of Paul parting with the elders of Ephesus, as recorded in chapter nine of the Acts of the Apostles."

AFRICAN SUPERSTITION.

The poor ignorant Kafirs and Fingoes of South Africa have a belief in the existence of a being whom they call "Tikoloshe," and who, they say, lives at the bottom of the river, where he has a house, a garden, and large flocks and herds.

They say that the Iguana, which is a great lizard, which they call "Xam," is his horse, and he rides it when he comes to the surface of the water. This being, "Tikoloshe," they describe as a little man about two feet high; and they say that he comes into their huts sometimes by night to steal their Indian corn, pumpkins, and other eatables; but that when they are awoke by the noise, a mist comes before their eyes, and they cannot see him. But occasionally they catch a glimpse of him outside, just as he is returning to the river.

Many of the children at Heald Town would not, by night, go near the little stream that runs in the valley there, for fear of Tikoloshe catching them!

THE WORLD RESTORED.

This world was once a paradise;
When will it be again?
When sin shall have its overthrow
And righteousness shall reign;
When sea and shore, hill, plain, and dell,
Shall own thy power, Emanuel!

Who could look on this universe,
Its ever-varied face,
Its beautiful sublimities,
And every softer grace,—
And not confess how passing fair,
Had evil never entered there?

The glories of the summer noon,
The splendour of the beam,
The night's more gentle loveliness,
The moon's delicious gleam,
The woods, the waters,—each have shone
With countless beauties of their own.

But how hath man with wickedness
The lovely scene defiled!
War, Rapine, Murder, Cruelty,
Transformed it to a wild;
And hateful spirits spread their wing,
Like fiends in Eden revelling.

Bring back this world, Great Conqueror!
To thy benignant sway;
Establish Truth in Righteousness,
And haste the Gospel-day;
Then might we hope this earth to see
As like to heaven as earth could be.

THE NAMACQUA CLASS-LEADER'S ANSWER TO PRAYER.

MEETING a class for tickets one day, the native leader (Job Whitboy) related the following circumstance:—

"The other day (said he) I lost my spectacles. I sought diligently, but could not find them anywhere. I was greatly distressed at the loss, for I cannot read my Bible without spectacles; and *ik kan niet klaar kom zonder God's woord.*

I prayed to God about the matter, asking Him to help me, for I was in great trouble. Well, I had no sooner got up from my knees, and gone out of the house, than I found my spectacles lying on the path; I picked them up, put them into my pocket, and went on my way with joy, such as I think I never had before."

AFRICAN LOVE FOR THE SCRIPTURES.

A *Griqua* man (Abram Kok) comes to ask the Missionary if he can procure a *Bible.*

Missionary—"I have not a *new* one that I can give you. I have a second-hand one, but it is *old.*"

Man.—"Oh, that is nothing. If the *book* is old, *the word is new.*"

A TOUR FOR LITTLE FOLKS ROUND A LITTLE ISLAND IN SAMOA.

MY DEAR CHILDREN,—

Shall I tell you something about a tour for little folks round a little island?

Oh yes, you say: who are the tourists, and where is the little island, and tell us all about it? Very well, so I will. It was not a picnic to some pretty place. No; we were not so gay of heart as that. It was not only to see the little island, and admire the pretty fishes, or to gather lovely coral specimens. No, we might do so, perhaps, for the little folks another day. Well, then, what brought about the tour? Do you see that little girl there, pale as marble, in the arms of the native nurse? How poorly she looks, dear child.

Her name is Mary Grace, or Polly, as we now call her. She has been ill for months, and doctors are far away: Missionaries know the want of them often; but they are far, far away. The Lord, however, is at hand, and He is better than a thousand. Poor Polly seems to get no better with medicine, so we thought we would take our boat, and five natives, this morning, and have a sail, and try what fresh air would do for the dear little girl.

Now, you would like to know the name of the little island: it is Manono. A precious emerald of an island is this Manono to look at, as green as a melon, and "as gay as a lark." The mild and merry trade-wind was blowing over it as the Mission-house clock struck eight. The boat is launched, and the sister and brother of little Polly are all ready; so now away we go.

Here we are, all of us snugly seated beneath the awning; and, after a tumble on this side and then on that, our sailor-boy has got the sail set. The towns of Matasiva, Lepuiai, and Aaeno fly behind us, like mile-stones on a railroad, until we have now lost the wind. There is the island fortress of Apolimo right ahead of us, outside the reef, and away beyond it to the westward, running up far away among the clouds, is proud Savaii, the island pyramid of a thousand years.

grand and beautiful indeed. But here's a village we are passing, called Apai. A chief of Apai, Mamone, as he was named, was a good man, but he was drowned one day while fishing alone off Manono, his native village. Here is an old Missionary station. Up the side of the slope there, beneath a grove of orange and citron-trees, side by side, in nameless graves, lie the Missionary and his wife, who lived and laboured in this village for many years, and are now waiting for the coming of the Lord. Though Apai is a little village, yet the Saviour began the great work there which has long since spread into every family on Manono. But our boat glides along. Sweeping round a point of land, we now come right against the wind, which was before shut off by the island. Every one now to the paddles, and luff the boat. There now, splashing, plunging, we go through the crested little breakers, running round this point of land and then round that, until we reach Falemoa, a small offshoot of a village, scarcely worth more than its name, which means a fowl-house. Two fishing-nets are suspended there along a line of cocoa-nut trees, so you are sure what trade the people follow.

But how is Polly now, you would like to know. Look there, she has gone to sleep on her mamma's lap and her little brother Tom is nodding round to everybody, rather nappish too. We won't awake the dear children: let them sleep on. The wind is gently fanning the feverish brow of our dear little invalid, while the boat is ploughing away towards the point Matautu. The wind is conquered, and now it shall serve us. Unfurl, the sail and steer to the right, and away we fly. Here is Salua on the starboard; there are houses plenty: they have not a window nor a door — nothing save posts and thatched roofs above them, with here and there a dwelling enclosed with the split bamboo. Roofs you see, as round and conical as ricks of corn, and not much higher: only a few are oblong, in Tongan style. There you see a chapel, and yonder is another, neither of them good enough, yet ours alone is large enough for the whole village on a Sunday.

Away we glide along on the shallow sea, with the wind abaft. Salua is passed, and there is Satoi, a tribe of daring heathens until lately, and the last town on Manono where the dull, long beat for the dark night-dance was heard on the little island. One of our crew is a convert belonging to that place.

The servant who is baling the boat is a Saluan. She has this moment pitched the baler overboard, and away she plunges after it, as a dog would have done after his master's hat. A few minutes, and she is on board again, laughing heartily at her adventure. But there's the Mission house, our home, in a grove of bread-fruit trees. Don't you think it would make a pretty picture? Nicely elevated above the sea, looking to the sunrise, snow-white, plastered, wattled walls, overshadowed with verandah, windows, doors, all right, though roughly done by hands unused to handle tools. From the boat here I am sure it would please you in a picture, if taken in the clear, bright light we have to-day. Here, then, our tour is ended, two hours and twenty minutes from the time we started: so now you shall guess the size of the island on which little Polly and her sister and brother were born. Perhaps we may say something else about the little folks some other day.

MARTYN DYSON.

Precept.

THIS IS HIS COMMANDMENT, THAT WE SHOULD BELIEVE ON THE NAME OF HIS SON JESUS CHRIST. I *John*. iii. 23.

Promise.

BELIEVE ON THE LORD JESUS CHRIST, & THOU SHALT BE SAVED.

Acts. XVI. 31.

Prayer.

LORD SAVE US: WE PERISH.

Matt. VIII. 25.

BREAD MAKING IN SAMOA.

SAMOAN MASI.

My dear Children,—

I wonder if you ever heard of Samoan Masi? Perhaps you have heard the word "masi" before, or you may have read it in that charming book called, "Fiji, and the Fijians." There it means native cloth; but with us it means native bread. Perhaps you ask, "Is Samoan bread different from our kind of bread?" If you will go with me this morning

I will show you how the natives in Samoa make it, and then you shall tell me what you think of it.

Here, then, away we go. Do you see those two boys who are digging away there like miners. One is called Peletisala, and the other is a namesake of Mr. Benson; but he cannot pronounce his own name, so we will call him Penisoni. Though neither is above eighteen years of age, they have been meeting in class, as we Methodists say, for several years. They were both proposed as local preachers a month ago, but it was thought that they were too young. The Spirit of God is at work on the minds of young persons here, you see, much in the same way as elsewhere. The tallest boy was a wild-looking little fellow when I first saw him, with his face blackened with soot in a most funny manner.

But, about the masi. The boys have now finished the pit. It was really hard work to break through that piece of a rock. Manono is an islet of rocks, so that you can't make masi pits everywhere. Is that the size they make them? Oh, no; very few are so small. They often make them some dozen feet across, and many of them are five feet deep, and as round as a barrel.

Do you see the girls. Pray what are they about? That one is arranging a bundle of banana leaves, taking off strips from the leaf-stalks to make them pliable. This merry, laughing, careless creature on the side of the masiputis is plaiting the branches of the cocoa-nut tree into long and narrow mats, which she calls laupola. Yonder is a little clever Tongan boy, of twelve years of age, cutting iofi, or double wooden pegs, or native pincers. There, again, you see a young man, a native of Manono, running up and down the bread-fruit trees like a sailor among the rigging of a ship. One by one he is bringing down a shower of bread-fruit with his "lou"—a rod with a crook at the end, and long enough for a fishing-rod. Away flies Penisoni to the bush, and is back again quick as a lamplighter, almost lost in a burden of grass. Here, then, every thing is ready, and now for the lining of the luaimasi. They put grass first. That's the masi bed, all nice and dry as a bird's nest. Next comes the "laupola," (the mats) as green as grass. This is neatly laid and pinned in tiers from the top to the bottom of the pit. Next comes the long and broad banana leaves. These are carefully suspended in large numbers round the sides of the pit, with the leaf-stalk upwards, and the dressing is finished.

Now for the next thing. Here's the bread-fruit in heaps. Some of the fruit is thirty inches in circumference, and nearly as round as an orange. A fine fruit, is it not—quite a meal of itself? But is that masi? Wait a little, and you shall see. The girl has just brought a bucket of water and a toipua, or little wooden hatchet of a very primitive kind. Her first work is to cleave the fruit round the stalk with the toipua, without separating the parts; and after passing it through the water, it is pitched into the pit. Now for another, and another, and another, till there is a hundred fruit cast into this small luaimasi, and piled up also above the pit, like apples on a stall. There, you may call that the flour out of which the native bread is made. The tub will now be closed; but first they throw the soft stem of the banana-tree over the fruit. That is intended to soften and moisten it. The stalks of the banana leaves are now gathered carefully up, and folded, and fastened over the fruit, until it is thoroughly protected from the rain. Fresh, loose banana leaves are now spread over the whole, and these again are buried beneath a dozen or two old baskets of "laupola," and a bed of leaves, all of which are now pressed down by heavy stones. In about a fortnight they will open it again, and throw in other ripe bread-fruit, and then leave the whole tightly closed up to dissolve, and melt, and ferment into a mass of masi. You may then call it dough. The natives will then take it from the pit as they want it, and, after baking it to their fancy, they will enjoy it as you would a bun. Say, now, what do you think of Samoan masi? Let us also adore our Father who is in heaven, who giveth food to all flesh.

MARTYN DYSON.

A HOTTENTOT FABLE.

A GENTLEMAN has collected a number of Hottentot legends, comprising seven ghost stories, four accounts of men or animals, eleven household tales, one legend, and one fable. The materials for the book were original manuscripts in the library of Sir George Grey. Here is a specimen of the stories :—

"A Dutchman was walking by himself, and saw a snake lying under a large stone. The snake implored his help; but when she had become free, she said, 'Now I shall eat you.'

"The man answered, 'That is not right. Let us first go to the hare.'

"When the hare had heard the affair, he said, 'It is right.'

"'No,' said the man; 'let us ask the hyæna.'

"The hyæna declared the same, saying, 'It is right.'

"'Now let us at last ask the jackal,' said the man in despair.

"The jackal answered very slowly and considerately, doubting the whole affair, and demanding to see first the place, and whether the man was able to lift the stone. The snake lay down, and the man, to prove the truth of his account, put the stone again over her.

"When she was fast, the jackal said, 'Now let her lie there.'"

WORK WHILE IT IS CALLED DAY.

We are living, we are dwelling
In a grand and awful time;
In an age on ages telling—
To be living is sublime!

Will ye play, then, will ye dally
Hear ye not the call divine?
Up! it is Jehovah's rally!
God's own arm hath need of thine!

Worlds are charging, heaven beholding;
Thou hast but an hour to fight:
Now, the blazoned cross unfolding,
On, right onward for the right!

On! let all the soul within you
For the truth's sake go abroad;
Strike! let every nerve and sinew
Tell on ages, tell for God!

I

AM THE LORD:

THAT IS MY NAME:

AND MY GLORY

WILL I NOT GIVE TO

ANOTHER, NEITHER

MY

PRAISE TO GRAVEN

IMAGES.

ISAIAH, xlii. 8.

A KAFIR SUPERSTITION.

THE Kafirs and Fingoes have a singular belief in a power residing in streams and rivers. I will call it *the spirit of the waters.* They believe that this spirit has the power of *calling* people. A Kafir, in his house, or his field, or perhaps when in conversation with others, all at once imagines himself "*called by the river.*" He immediately rushes down to the water, and, according to the impression he there receives, either casts himself into the stream, or kills an ox or a goat on the bank, and throws all the flesh into the water.

A case occurred not very long ago, at one of the stations in British Kaffraria. A Kafir girl was seen rushing impetuously to the river. Some people tried to detain her, but she would not be hindered, declaring that "the river had called her." She was never heard of afterwards.

They believe further that the *spirit of the waters* has the power of inflicting diseases upon those who refuse to obey the call.

Once when I was travelling with my interpreter, near Mount Coke, my interpreter entered into conversation with a boy whose face was much disfigured by an eruption. He said to the boy, "What is the matter with your face?" "Oh! it's the river!" was the reply. "What do you mean? How can the river make your face so?" "Are you such a fool as not to know about the spirit of the river?" said the boy, "Once that river was *very strong;* people could not play with it then. But now so much soap is put into it by the Christians washing their clothes there, that it is not so strong as it was; but you see in my face what it can do!"

SIERRA LEONE.

CUTTING DOWN A FETISH-TREE.

"The Fetish" in West Africa is the demon worshipped by the people, and greatly held in awe by them. The "fetish-tree" is a tree set apart by the natives for their idolatrous worship.

The one in the picture was at Waterloo, in the colony of Sierra Leone, and was kept by one of the Yorubans residing there. It was a cotton-tree, which bears a substance somewhat similar to the ordinary cotton imported from abroad. Such fetish-trees are decorated with old rags, feathers, skulls of sheep and goats, pieces of old iron, and all kinds of rubbish. The one in question was adorned in this way, and had been worshipped by the people for many years. The Missionary in charge of the station, thus describes its destruction :—

"A party of professing Christians, of the Yoruba tribe, came to tell me that they were going to cut down their fetish-tree, being determined to worship it no more. A rope was fixed to the trunk, and the work of destruction then began. Such a pulling down of refuse, which had been hung upon the tree, then took place! Old garments, the bones and skulls of animals, &c., all hung up in honour of the fetish. The owner stood by all the time in solemn silence, as if he were wondering how it was that his god could suffer such a destruction to take place.

"When the tree fell a loud shout arose from the people who stood near. Many others, however, through superstitious fear, remained at a distance, and beheld the scene afar off.

MAGGIE AND HER NURSE.

A STORY OF CHINA.

It was at noon on the first day of the new year we had to part with our little Maggie. Only three more days, and she would be six and a half years old. We shall always call her *little Maggie*, because she has now gone to that bright land where little children never grow old.

What a happy new-year's day was that for our little Maggie; but what a sad, sad day for her parents, her little brother, who then lost his only playmate, and for all of us who loved her so much! Maggie was a bright sunbeam in that Missionary home. It was not so much her happy, smiling face and merry voice, as because she was always so gentle, so good, and so kind to her younger brother, and to all the little Chinese children around her.

We all loved her because she loved Jesus, and wanted to be like Him. Maggie used often to sing, "I want to be an angel, and with the angels stand." In the early morning we would hear her sweet voice singing, "There is a happy land, far, far away," or "I'm going home to die no more." Maggie had never been to the Sabbath-school to learn to sing those beautiful songs. No; where she lived such a thing as a Sabbath-school had never been known: her home was far on the other side of the world from you—away off in China. It was Maggie's mamma who had taught her to sing so many pretty songs and hymns for children; the same ones, too, that you know and sing. Almost every afternoon you might have seen Maggie sitting in her low rocking-chair, by her mother's side, reading about Jesus Christ from her New Testament, the one her papa gave her for her own, and wrote her name in it for her. After the reading lesson was finished, her work-box was brought out, and, while learning to sew, she wanted to be singing those sweet songs, or else listening while her mamma read aloud "that sweet story of old," or, perhaps, "stories of Bible-men." Though Maggie never had the privilege of going to Sabbath-school, yet she had a share in one treat which many Sabbath-school children enjoy. She, too, had some nice books. What a treasure they were! Such beautiful pictures, such nice stories, every word of which she could understand herself.

Maggie had been very ill for two weeks. Her throat was so sore and painful she could not talk much, and by and by she could only speak in a whisper. If spoken to, she would always try to smile a little, to let us see she had heard us, and loved us still. When her mamma told her she was very sick, she said, "Yes, I know it. I am not afraid to die. I'll go and be one of Jesus' little lambs. I shall see my little brother and sister in heaven." Before Maggie was sick at all, when talking of her relatives in America, and telling the names of those who had often sent her little presents, and of those she most loved she would turn and say—"But Jesus is sweetest of all, isn't He, mamma?" Maggie's nurse was an old Chinese woman, who had taken care of her ever since she was a little baby. This poor woman had for more than six years heard about Jesus Christ, who loved her, and died to save her soul; but she did not care at all for that, or love Him in return: no; she loved her wooden idols better.

Maggie, in saying her prayers, always remembered to pray for her Ama, as the nurse was called in Chinese. Not long before Maggie's death, as she was naming three whom she expected to be with her in heaven, she said, "and my Ama will be there, too." When little Maggie died, the Ama wept bitterly. She did not cry with a great noise, though, as many of these poor heathen do, so as to have people think they are very sorry. She was often seen to weep; and though she still did all her work as faithfully as ever, yet we could see she was telling the truth when she said, "I have no *heart* in my work now."

Years before, when Maggie's little brother died, the Ama, like all Chinese, had been afraid to stay in the room where his body lay; but now she was found alone, weeping over her dear Maggie's cold form. When the Ama was told how Maggie had long been praying for her—praying she might love her dear Jesus—her heart was melted with grief. Not long after, she said, "I have made up my mind as to what I shall do." From that time the Ama has seemed a changed person. She loves now to talk about Jesus, loves to attend family-worship, and loves to go to preaching. Though her eyes are old, and she is near-sighted, yet she is learning to read.

You should see her putting on her glasses, and then carrying her little catechism up close to the window that she might be able to see to pick out the Chinese characters, which are so difficult to learn. How fast she is learning now! A few months ago she had to be asked to bring her book and read; now she comes book in hand, and, with such a pleasant look, says, "I would like to read a little now, if you are not too busy." Then, two or three lines was all she could learn at once; now, a whole half-page is not too long a lesson. To think of an old woman nearly sixty, who had never sung in all her life before, beginning now to learn to sing, "Happy Land" and other tunes her little pet used to sing so sweetly. You would never imagine the tune she sings, and those queer-sounding words, were meant for "Happy Land" the "Happy Land" you all know so well. It is music to her ear, though, and so she sings away. We all love this good old Ama more than ever before, not only for our little Maggie's sake, but because she is trying to serve our dear and blessed Saviour.

My dear little friends, is there not some one whom you love, but who does not yet love Jesus? Will you not begin to-night to pray for that one? If you really wish with all your heart to meet that person in heaven, God will hear your prayer, as he heard Maggie's for her Ama.—*Foreign Missionary.*

CURIOUS SOUTH-AFRICAN SUPERSTITION.

The native tribes generally have a notion that there exists a strange species of snake, which frequents moist places, such as the vicinity of fountains and rivers, and differs from all other reptiles, both in its general character, and in its capacity to injure man. It is only to be seen in the night-time, and that very rarely. It is sixteen or eighteen feet long, and about five inches thick. And it carries on its head two lights, which it is able to leave at pleasure on a given spot, while it goes to seek its prey by their assistance. They tell me that, before I came to reside at this station, (Wittebergen) one of these snakes frequented the fountain, or well, just below the Mission House; and that one night it stole a calf out of an adjoining kraal, and took it into a cave among the rocks. They have shewn me the entrance to the said cave, which is at first wide enough to admit a man, but narrows exceedingly, leading down to darkness, and appears not at all unlikely for the abode of some wild beast. A few nights ago, a young Masuto man, who was out searching for his horses near the upper fountains, saw (so he says) one of these formidable reptiles, lights and all; and he was so terrified that he took to his heels.

Many natives, whom I have asked, bear witness to having seen and heard of similar snakes in other localities. They say that when the snake moves, he makes a noise like the rattling of chains; and that if you offend him, he has the power to blast you with his breath; which, if it does not cause death, inflicts upon you some fearful bodily ailment. The heathen, when they go to drink water at a fountain, which has the notoriety of being frequented by one of these reptiles, use the precaution to take a little of the mud, and put a spot of it on each cheek, and on the forehead. This they believe to be a certain specific against his baneful influence. My young friends will, no doubt, be at a loss what to understand by so strange a superstition. I believe it to be "founded on fact;" but that the simple fact is, that the fountains and moist places spoken of are seen to be at times illuminated by the ignis-fatuus, or Will-o'-the-Wisp, called by some Jack-o'-Lantern, and that the "rattling of chains," poisonous breath, &c., are only erroneous notions, conceived under the influence of superstitious terror.

LETTER FROM A SCHOLAR IN INDIA TO MRS. CAMPBELL, A MISSIONARY'S WIFE IN ENGLAND.

"*Bangalore, Feb. 23d,* 1864.

"MY DEAR MOTHER,*—I have the opportunity of writing these few lines to you, in hopes of finding you and Mr. Campbell in the enjoyment of perfect health, as it leaves us, thanks be to the providence of God for his merciful kindness towards us in keeping us so long with life and strength.

Dear mother, we have received your kind and loving letter, and we are very glad to hear that you are coming to Bangalore once more to see all your friends. Oh! how glad shall we be to see you in our land, therefore we have all prayed to God that He may bless you in all your ways, and guide you over that wide ocean.

Dear mother, I am very thankful to you for the description of Glasgow that you took so much trouble to write about. I wish I had been there, but I cannot see it, and so I must give it up; but there is a place where the weary are at rest, more beautiful, holy, and glorious—even heaven.

* The girls in Mrs. Campbell's school always call h "dear mother."

Dear mother, I pray God, day and night, after this life is passed, to receive me into that glorious kingdom. What a family there will be in heaven when we get there. Oh, it is a lovely home. Let us meet each other at the right hand of the Judge in that happy world, in the presence of the glorious Saviour: we long to join that glorious band and hear the music there. I have nothing to say particular about the church: only five heathens were converted after your departure. I think you will be glad to hear the glad tidings of the salvation of souls. May God guide them in this troublesome world, and help them to love the best Friend of all friends, and in the hour of sorrow to trust in the divine Comforter.

Dear mother, we must part in this earthly wilderness, but we shall never part in heaven, where our blessed Saviour is preparing a place for those only who are washed in the blood of the bleeding Lamb, who died on Mount Calvary. Our kind father, Mr. Rice, and his dear children, are in good health, but our dear mother, Mrs. Rice, has been very ill, but at present is a little better, by the tender mercy of God. Their daughter, went to England on the 6th January: our beloved father, Mr. Rice, went with her as far as to Madras. Oh, may God protect them in all their journey, and deliver them from the danger of that roaring ocean, and take them safely over its deep water! Dear mother, the last letter I wrote was my own words and handwriting. I did not ask any one to help me. Here I conclude my letter with humble thanks to you and Mrs. Campbell. I trust, if it contains many mistakes that you will excuse them.

"I beg to remain,

"Your obedient and affectionate daughter,

"Esther."

THE

WESLEYAN JUVENILE OFFERING.

OUT OF
THE MOUTHS OF
BABES AND SUCKLINGS
HAST THOU
ORDAINED PRAISE.

THE CHILD MISSIONARY.

A LESSON FROM HEATHEN LANDS.

"You have been long absent, my child," said a teacher in Fiji to a dear little Fijian girl about nine years of age.

"Yes, Sir," she replied, "I have been to Ruku-ruku to visit my mother's friends."

"But were you not afraid? Are they not all cannibals?"

"Not all, Sir; and they would not hurt me. I am not at all afraid of them."

"I trust that, when there, you try to do them good. Next time you go let me know, and I will give you some books; and you must teach them to read, and to say the Lord's Prayer, &c."

"Oh, Sir, they can read small words, and they know the Lord's Prayer, the Confession, and Thanksgiving (Te Deum): I have taught them so far; but they have no Gospels to read."

"And have you prayed with them?"

"Oh yes; I prayed with them every day, morning and evening.

Her teacher's heart filled to overflowing, and he remembered that "Out of the mouths of babes and sucklings hast thou ordained praise."

Little Harriet was not long before she found an opportunity for sending the books supplied by her teacher: they were eagerly sought after by these so lately degraded cannibals.

Local preachers were instructed to go and preach to them; and very soon they sent a request that a teacher might be sent to live with them, that they might receive instruction continually.

This dear child obeyed our Saviour's injunction, "Let your light so shine before men that they may see your good works, and glorify your Father which is in heaven."

May you and I, dear reader "*So* let our light shine." We may not have the honour of introducing the knowledge of our Saviour's name into an heathen village; but by faithfully performing our duties, we may be little Missionaries wherever we are.

ALL THE ENDS

OF THE

EARTH

HAVE SEEN THE

SALVATION

OF OUR

GOD.

PSALM xcviii. 3.

THE LITTLE ITALIAN.

An English lady had stopped at a hotel in Naples, that large and noisy city of Italy, situated on the beautiful bay which bears its name, on the opposite side of which rises up Mount Vesuvius, the ever-burning mountain. It was a lovely scene that was there presented at that early hour of the morning, when the brilliant sun, not yet come forth in its full strength, threw its softer beams upon the sparkling waters.

While occupied in gazing at the beautiful prospect, a soft voice and light step interrupted the lady's meditations, and a little girl, of about nine years old, who had knocked at the outer door without being heard, gently entered the room, with a small basket on her arm, and, bidding the lady "Good morning" in the Italian language, told her that she had brought her back some linen she had given to be washed. The lady smiled at the child as she took the clothes, and gave her a piece of money for herself.

Instead of retiring in silence, as a little English girl would probably have done, the Italian child stood and gazed upon the English lady, whose light-coloured hair and eyes, being so different from those seen in the girl's own country, appeared to fill her with wonder and interest.

"The lady is beautiful," she said at last, with a look of innocent admiration; "beautiful hair! beautiful eyes!"

"My child," said the English lady, smiling kindly at her, "my hair and eyes are not beautiful in England."

"Oh! they are beautiful in Naples," said the child; but directly changing the expression of her face, her own dark eyes assumed a more earnest and anxious look, as she asked, in her sweet native voice and manner, "Is the lady a foreigner?"

"Yes, I am English," was the answer.

"English!" said the Italian child, and cast down her eyes, which seemed to speak without words, so plainly did they express each changing sentiment of her young mind.

There was a silence, and the lady had moved away, when she heard the gentle, earnest voice again. The little Italian girl stood beside her with her eyes raised in deep interest to her face, and, bending forward with a natural and expressive movement, said, in a tone that showed anxiety for the reply, "Does the Signora (lady) believe in God, the great God," she added, with a light motion of the hands towards the fair scene beyond the windows, "the great God who made all things? does the signora believe in the great God?"

The lady was surprised, and even affected at such a question, and at the deep earnestness of the young speaker.

"Yes, my child," she replied, "I do believe in God."

"Oh! that is good," cried the child: "the lady is English, but she believes in God."

She was silent for a moment, as if in reflection, but yet did not seem to be satisfied. She drew nearer to the English lady, and with her little hands joined together and pressed upon her breast, and her expressive eyes fastened in deep earnestness on her face, she asked again, "But the good Saviour Jesus Christ; oh! He is good; He is the Redeemer of our souls; does the lady believe in the good Saviour?"

With a tear almost springing to her eye, the lady answered, "Yes, dear child, I do believe in the good Saviour Jesus Christ: He is good; He died for us; his blood cleanses from all sin."

"Oh yes! He is good," cried the little girl: "the lady believes in the good Saviour."

Again there was a silence, and the Italian girl continued to gaze upon the English lady, and seemed puzzled by some thoughts which she could not clear up to herself. The lady, too, surprised and pleased by the interest which the little stranger showed in her, was occupied in endeavouring to trace its source.

The child spoke again, and this time in a still more doubtful voice, as if she had been thinking, and had at last found out what it was which the English stranger might not believe in. "But the holy mother," ("la santa madre,") said she in a more trembling manner, "does the lady believe in her?"

"My child," said the lady, "you mean, without doubt the mother of our Lord Jesus Christ, the Virgin Mary. You ask me, do I believe in her? Yes; I believe that such a blessed woman lived, and that God chose her to be the mother of our blessed Saviour's human nature; and the Bible tells us that she was thus 'highly favoured among women,' and that is nearly all we are told about her; but I believe that she is now with God, and with her Saviour, and with all those whom He has redeemed from sin and suffering."

"And the lady goes to church, and prays to the blessed virgin?" said the child with anxious eagerness.

"I go to church, dear child," said the lady, "but I do not pray to the blessed virgin, for the Virgin Mary was a woman like myself, though a better and holier one; but I do not pray to her, for we are told to pray to God through Christ only; and we are told to ask pardon of our offences through Him only; and we are told that God gave us one Saviour only, and that Saviour was his well-beloved Son; therefore I do not pray to the blessed virgin, nor to any other saint, but only ask God, for Christ's sake, to pardon me, and to instruct me, and to lead me in the way I should go."

The child looked very thoughtful. After a little she said, "The lady does not pray to the holy mother, but she believes in the good Saviour, she goes to the church and prays to the great God, and to the good Saviour; will she never pray to the holy mother?"

"No, dear child, for the mother of our Lord was a mere mortal woman like ourselves, and if I should pray to her I should make her equal to God, who alone is the hearer and answerer of prayer."

The Italian child listened in silence, then suddenly seizing the English lady's hand, she pressed it to her lips, saying only, "The signora is good;" and she went away.

The English lady thought much of her afterwards. How unusual the interest which that little stranger took in her spiritual state! She had heard, evidently, that England was a nation of heretics; she believed, like many other devout and ignorant people in Roman Catholic countries, that Protestants had no faith in God, or in Christ, and were no better than infidels. Thus arose her concern and anxiety to know that lady's belief; and how sweetly, how tenderly was it expressed!

Poor little girl! brought up in a land of superstition and bigotry, she is taught to believe in many things which God's word does not authorize. Yet may we not learn a lesson from her, of deep concern for superstitious Romanists, unbelieving Jews, and ignorant idolaters?

Perhaps this remembrance of the little Italian girl may not be useless to some more favoured English child.

S. B.

SNAKE WORSHIP.

It is not a little singular that the odious and venomous race of serpents should ever become the objects of human adoration.

It is well known that all tropical countries are infested with snakes. Towards the end of the summer season, but especially during the rain, serpents issue out of their holes, and do great mischief to men and animals. In Bengal, hundreds of persons die every year of the bite of the snake. Hence, on many occasions throughout the year, the dreaded Manasa Devi, the Queen of the Snakes, is propitiated by presents, vows, and religious rites. In the month of Shrábana the worship of the snake goddess is celebrated with great honour. Men, women, and children, all offer presents on the occasion, to avert from themselves the wrath of the terrific deity. . . .

"Bengali mothers, anxious for the preservation of their children from the bite of serpents, implore the favour of Manasa. On one of the last days of Shrábana, women may be seen coming out of a village with vessels in their hands, containing a composition of rice, milk, and sugar. Proceeding out of the village, they take their station generally near a tank, and offer their homely present to the goddess on behalf of their children. The presentation being done, they help themselves to the rice, milk, and treacle."

These remarks will prepare our friends for the scene which is represented in the picture, viz. the worship of the living snake. On the occasion to which we have referred, when the queen of the snakes is worshipped in India at the yearly festival, live snakes —even the huge boa-constrictor and the deadly cobra

—are introduced. Their fangs, however, having been carefully extracted, no harm ensues.

The Rev. Dr. Doran mentions that he had met with a family in the Cochin country who were in the habit of making a household god of the very dangerous snake called the cobra-di-capello. It dwelt on the premises where they resided, and was served with daily offerings of food by each member of the family, while, at the same time, its power as a divinity was regarded with uncommon awe.

It happened that one day a native girl, one of the children of the family, of about ten years of age, was bitten by it; and Dr. Doran, in the course of his visits to the people, approached the dwelling just as she had breathed her last. The bite of this kind of snake, it is believed, is nearly always fatal. On hearing the cause of the poor girl's death, the Missionary asked if they had killed the snake; and he relates, that never will he forget the expression of the countenance of the mother of the deceased when she replied, "Sir, if we were to kill the cobra, which is still about the house, all the other members of my family would die likewise." "The fact was," as Dr. Doran adds, "that the animal was to them in the place of God, and was worshipped by them, and was regarded by them, as God."

THE JUBILEE TREE.

God hath the basket blessed,
  And multiplied the store;
Oh! be His name confessed
  On ev'ry land and shore!
Once a tender germ was planted,
  Now a mighty tree hath grown;
For God his grace hath granted,
  And reared it for his own.

They are pass'd, the sires that set it,
  Pass'd, the eyes that watch'd it spread;
But shall we, their sons, forget it,
  Now that fifty years have fled?
Nay; in Christian love combining,
  Let us gather round the tree,
And with hearts and hands be joining
  To keep its Jubilee.

Oft have its leaves been wafted
  On India's balmy gales;
Oft on Ocean's isles have grafted,
  Or in Piedmont's gentle dales;
'Neath Afric's shadeless burning,
  'Mid the ice of Labrador,
'Mid Italia's darkened learning,
  Or China's fabled lore.

Oh! sweet indeed our gladness
  As our Jubilee we keep,
If those leaves shall cheer some sadness,
  Or dry some eyes that weep;
If some foot that far is wandering,
  Be turned towards heaven above;
And some stony heart be pondering
  On the depths of Jesus' love.

THE TWO DEATHS.

"We have just had two deaths on our station, which have been a cause of comfort to us," says a Missionary in South Africa, and our Christian friends in England will praise God for his goodness to his redeemed creatures in heathen lands.

The old woman going home.

An old woman died who had spent the greater part of her days in heathenism. Just before her last illness she began to seek the Lord, came twice to the inquirers' class, and was then taken sick; but the Spirit carried on the work at home, and she found "peace and joy in believing." She refused to take the medicine her friends offered her, saying she did not want to live; her Father had called her, and she wanted to go home.

The child going to Jesus.

One little girl in the school, when near death, sent for several of her companions, and asked them to sing a hymn about Jesus; "because," said she, "I am going to live with Him, and I want to sing his praise."

STORIES FROM SOUTH AFRICA.

The Missionary who has sent us these little stories about the Namacquas of South Africa, where he is living, says that they illustrate the character and habits of the people about him. I am sure it must be very disagreeable to live among such greedy, covetous people.

"A man from a distance comes to see us: he is a stranger.

After having shaken hands, he sits down on the ground, though there is a chair close by him.

He then asks for some tea, as he is weary with his journey.

Missionary answers, "We have not come here to supply the people with food, but to preach the word of God. You must go to the *trader*, and purchase."

However, we give him a cup of tea, as we were then at our evening meal.

He now sits a little without speaking. Then asks, "Will you give me a pipe full of *tobacco?*"

Missionary—"We never give to persons who beg."

He then sits a little longer, and, when he sees nothing to be got, takes his hat, and walks away."

A person comes to ask the use of the Society's blacksmiths' and carpenters' shops, as there is a person come who can repair his waggon.

Missionary—"I will speak a word with you before I answer your question. Though I have been on this station nearly two years, yet you have not to this day given a contribution to the Society, great or small. When you are in need of any thing—*tools, medicine, counsel,* &c.—you come to the Missionary for it, but you never give any thing to the support of the Mission. Were I to do with *you* as you do to the *Mission,* I should refuse the use of the shops. But I do not do so. I only want you to look at your own conduct. You can use the shops; but I ask you, is such conduct right?"

Man.—"No, it is *not* right. But I intend to give something."

THE FAREWELL.

Speed Thy servants, Saviour, speed them!
Thou art Lord of winds and waves;
They were bound, but Thou hast freed them;
Now they go to free the slaves:
Be Thou with them!
'Tis Thine arm alone that saves.

Friends and home and all forsaking,
Lord! they go at Thy command
As their stay Thy promise taking,
While they traverse sea and land;
Oh be with them!
Lead them safely by the hand!

Speed them through the mighty ocean,
In the dark and stormy day,
When the waves, in wild commotion,
Fill all others with dismay:
Be Thou with them!
Drive their terrors far away.

When they reach the land of strangers,
And the prospect dark appears;
Nothing seen but toils and dangers,
Nothing felt but doubts and fears;
Be Thou with them!
Hear their sighs, and count their tears.

MISSIONARY NEWS.

You will be pleased to hear, dear young friends, that two ladies have just left England to go to foreign lands to teach the children there.

HELP FOR INDIA.

One is gone to Bangalore, in the East Indies, to keep a school for the daughters of Christian people, the children of European parents. There has been no school for them, and if they wished to learn they were obliged to go to a Roman Catholic school, and the nuns used to try and persuade them to be Papists. We hope the school will prosper, that the children will be diligent in their learning, and that they will be very kind to the lady who has left her home and friends to go to them.

A TEACHER FOR NATAL.

The other teacher is gone to South Africa, to a Mission station among the Kaffirs, called Edendale. There will be plenty of work for her to do, for the children on this station will be taught a great many things—how to read and work, and to keep themselves clean.

The mothers of the children want teaching too, they have had no one to tell them how to take proper care of their children or their houses.

NEWS FROM CHINA.

Miss Broxholme went to China at the end of last year to take charge of a Chinese school in Canton. She writes and says she thinks that she shall be very happy there, and that the Chinese girls are worthy of her affection. The Chinese language, she says, is certainly very difficult, but the barriers which seem so formidable are beginning to break down.

THE DYING TEACHER.

There was a young lady who went to the school at Canton before Miss Broxholme; Miss Gunson was her name, but she was taken ill, and obliged to come home to England. A few months ago she died—died happy in Jesus. She never regretted that she had gone to China to work for Christ. When dying, her father and mother stood by her bedside, watching her. She smiled very sweetly, and her sister asked her the reason. She replied, "It is Jesus." By and by they asked her, "Is Jesus precious?" She summoned all her strength, and answered, "Very." Looking at her mother, who was kneeling at her bedside, she said, "Mamma, pray." These were her last words, and she passed away to be for ever with the Lord. "And so He giveth his beloved sleep."

I have the pleasant news to tell you that many of our young friends, Sunday scholars and others, are helping us with making clothing and other things to send to the poor children in foreign lands, where clothing and money is scarce.

The children of Miss Howarth's Sunday-school class have sent a parcel of clothing.

From Miss Craig's, Inverury, Scotland, some nice useful and ornamental things have been sent; and a box of clothing from the Juvenile Sewing Society, Wainfleet.

Mrs. Barrett's and Mrs. Hellien's children have had a little bazaar at Richmond, and have got 18*l.*, to be sent to a school in Bangalore.

The young ladies in Miss Pipe's school have made clothing and subscribed money to send abroad.

We feel quite encouraged when we think of the interest our young friends take in the Mission work, and thank them most heartily for their symyathp and help.

THE

WESLEYAN JUVENILE OFFERING.

PERILS OF AFRICAN TRAVEL.

OUR young friends will like to read an account which Mrs. Bertram has sent, of a journey she has taken with Mr. Bertram to a country Mission station. She says—

"The journey was not very agreeable, owing to the bad state of the roads. The ascent of the mountains is really dreadful!

Some parts almost incline to a perpendicular, one ledge of rocks lying upon another, so as to have the appearance of deep, irregular steps. In another part the road skirts the base of the mountain, showing a ravine below of great depth, where a stream is seen rippling over large and small stones. As we ascended the first formidable part of the mountain range, the oxen gave way, and would not take to the yoke, despairing, as it were, of accomplishing the heavy task before them. The front oxen, having turned suddenly towards the waggon, caused confusion among all the rest; consequently the oxen nearest the waggon could not maintain their footing on such steep ground.

We soon felt our position to be dangerous, as the waggon was going backward down the declivity, and pulling the oxen with it. Mr. Bertram hastened to stop it by putting stones to the wheels, in which act he was almost run over. Seeing that all aid that could be given was required, I ran forward, stick in hand, to assist the driver. He was endeavouring to relieve one of the principal hind oxen, which, having got its head twisted back in an awkward position, was in danger of being strangled. After a few moments' perseverance he succeeded in extricating the poor animal.

At this crisis two strange men came to our assistance; and with some fresh arrangements a second attempt was made successfully.

Then followed one heavy ascent after another, the men inciting the poor oxen to pull by loud shouts and the free use of the whip. We toiled up on foot till we reached the summit of the hill. I may call this the cruel part of our way; it is impossible to ride up. Here the strangers left, with hearty thanks from us for their timely assistance, without which we had every prospect of being benighted.

Proceeding on our way, still rough and bad, we were met by some natives from the station, who had thoughtfully brought oxen to pull the waggon up the steep parts; as, however, we had got over the worst, we did not avail ourselves of the kind offer. Now, with a smooth road before us, we travelled along leisurely, and, arriving at the station about sunset, were welcomed by many smiling faces. The teacher's wife showed us into two little rooms, nicely white-washed. In this we were most agreeably surprised: the idea of sleeping in the waggon, ourselves and our children, in that cold dreary country, was not at all pleasant.

In the evening, several women came with the teacher's wife to visit us, expressing their delight at seeing me with the children once more among them. Being much fatigued by the day's journey, we retired to rest earlier than usual, and rose the next morning grateful to the Giver of every good gift for his continued mercies to us.

"After a very pleasant visit, our descent was threatened by a more narrow escape than that of our ascent. Coming down over those deep ledges of rocks at the base of the mountain, with an immediate fearful depth below, the oxen seemed to take fright at the terrible noise of the waggon behind them, as it jolted violently from one ledge to another. They suddenly made a terrific bolt on one side towards the frightful precipice: another step forward would have dashed all to pieces; but they were providentially stopped. A quick move from the driver, assisted by Mr. Bertram, brought all back to the road again, and very thankful we were to reach the bottom of this ugly mountain without any serious accident.

How often we are brought to experience and acknowledge that in God alone lies all our strength! Let His name be praised to all eternity!"

BE

NOT WEARY

IN

WELL DOING.

2 Thessalonians iii. 13.

"COME OVER, AND HELP US."

HARK ! a distant voice is calling ;
  Mournfully it meets the ear ;
Louder yet its accents falling,
  Fill each heart with solemn fear :
    Let us listen,
  As the woeful sound draws near.

'Tis the moan of millions dying ;
  Lost in sin's dark gloom they stay ;
'Tis the voice of wanderers crying,
  Ye who know the loving way,
    Come and guide us
  To the realm of perfect day.

We would help them, O our Father !
  Thou hast bid us freely give ;
Wilt Thou not the wand'rers gather,
  Bid their dying spirits live ?
    Hear our pleadings ;
  All our past neglect forgive.

We would send to every nation
  News of light and life divine ;
And to spread Thy free salvation,
  Now in youth we would combine ;
    Take these first-fruits,
  And let all our days be Thine.

WOULD YOU LIKE TO SEE JIM?

IN London there is a large building called Exeter Hall. It is used chiefly to hold religious meetings and anniversaries in. Once they were holding a Sabbath school anniversary there. A clergyman was addressing the children. He told them about two bad little boys, whom he had once known, and a good little girl, whom he afterwards learned to know. One day this little girl was going home from Sabbath school, where she had learned to try to be like Jesus, "who went about doing good." On her way home she saw two little boys, about her own age, quarrelling. She went up to them, and told them how wickedly they were acting. She made them stop quarrelling, and finally persuaded them to go to her Sabbath school. The boys were named Jim and Tom. The girl was called Mary Wood.

"Now, children," said the gentleman, "would you like to see Jim?"

With one voice they all shouted, "Yes."

"Jim, stand up," said the gentleman, looking to another part of the platform. A tall, reverend-looking gentleman, dressed in black, and wearing a white cravat, arose, and looked smilingly upon the children.

"There," said the speaker, "that is Jim. He has been a Missionary for several years in one of the South Sea Islands. Now would you like to see Tom?"

"Yes, yes, sir!" was heard all over the house.

"Here he is," said the speaker, straightening himself up; "he, too, has been a Missionary for years."

"And now, would you like to see little Mary Wood?"

"Yes, yes; oh yes!" burst forth in a perfect storm of voices.

"Well, do you see that lady over there, with a black velvet bonnet, putting down her veil, and blushing like a rose? That's little Mary Wood. And now I have a secret to tell you. *She is my wife!*" That good girl sowed a very little seed in God's garden. The fruit which it bore was two Missionaries to the heathen, with all the good resulting from their labours.—*From the Free Church of Scotland Children's Record.*

SNAKE-WORSHIP IN AFRICA.

It is not only in India that the snake is worshipped; the people of Africa consider the serpents as gods, and build temples for them.

The snake temple at Whydah, on the west coast of Africa, where serpent-worship is practised, is thus described by a Missionary:—

"It consists of a small circular building, about fifteen feet in diameter, having three entrances, and a pointed thatched roof. On entering this habitation of serpents, and looking abovehead, there were fifteen or twenty of these disgusting reptiles knotted around the poles forming the roof, whilst others were stretched at full length on the top of the wall.

"As we were leaving, a fetish woman entered with one of these loathsome objects of superstitious worship coiled round her neck, supporting its head and tail with either hand. As she approached the side of the building she elevated the head of the reptile, which stretched itself till it had gained the summit of the wall, where it speedily nestled itself among its compeers in veneration."

One can scarcely conceive of human nature as more sunk and debased than such a practice as this represents to us.

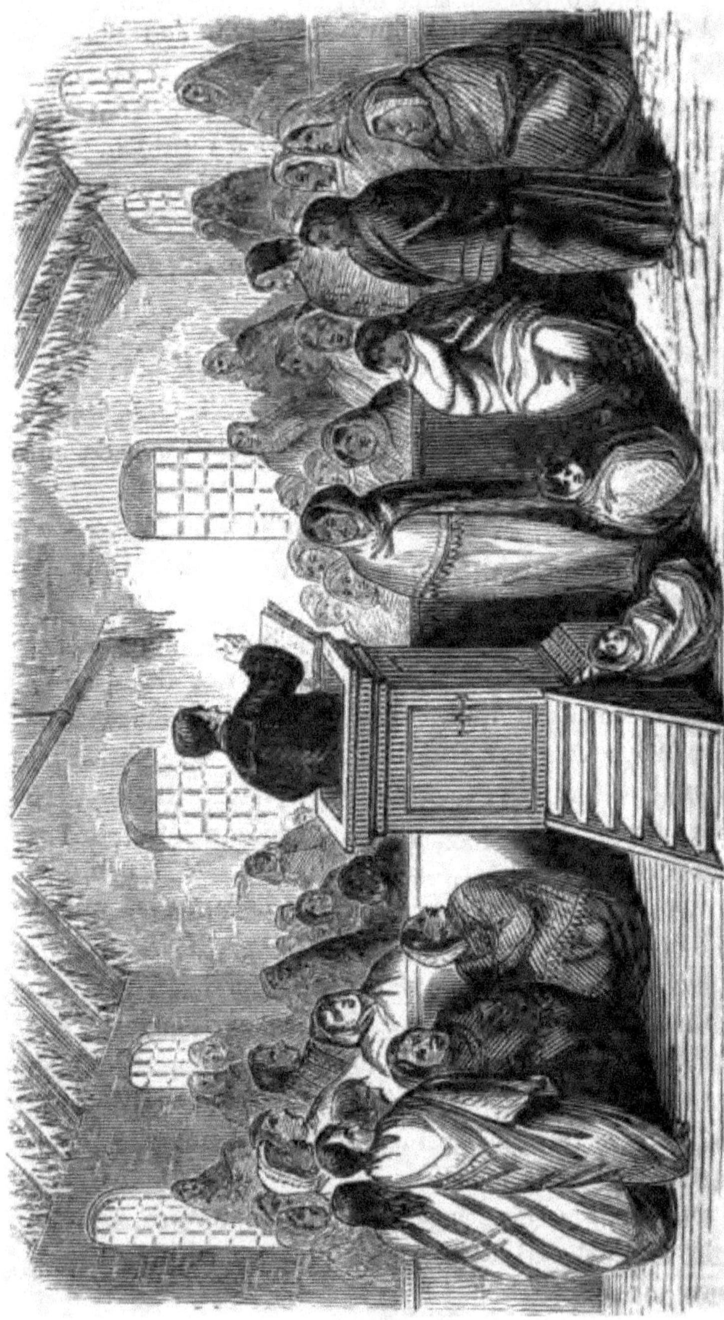

A WINTER CONGREGATION IN HUDSON'S BAY.

How should you like to go to chapel when the weather is so cold as it is where the Indians of Hudson's Bay live. The scene here represented is intended to shew the appearance which the winter congregations present in North-west America. It is very difficult, however, exactly to do this. There is no way of picturing the volume of breath, and the white frost arising from the breath on the eyebrows, whiskers, and hair of the people, and which gives a mass of faces an appearance which can never be shewn in a drawing. Besides this, there is the thick coating of glistening frost and snow on the walls, windows, and roofs, which gives the feeling of being in a temple of ice. Added to this, the muffled-up minister and people—the former scarcely able to speak a single word on account of the cold—are all incapable of adequate representation. The icicles hanging from the roof will be observed, with the stove-pipe passing through the wall.

It is a remarkable fact, and one of which our Missionary friends will delight to think, that, let the weather be what it may, the church is always full. The severest cold—the temperature being sometimes sixty, seventy, or even eighty degrees below the freezing point—does not prevent their attendance at the house of God. Neither do the heaviest rain, and the melting of the snow and ice, which render the country wet and muddy in the extreme, keep them from public worship on the Sabbath day.

When our Indian Missionary, the Rev. H. Budd, preached for the first time in this church, the interest and deep attention manifested by his fellow-countrymen was of the most striking character: they hung in breathless attention upon his lips.

A SHORT ACCOUNT OF ISRAEL.

WRITTEN BY HIS BROTHER SAMUEL.

Israel was the son of a native assistant Missionary of the Wesleyan Missionary Society. He was born at Bangalore on the 23rd of August 1845, and baptized by the Rev. Mr. Hardey.

The early religious training he received was blessed by the Lord, so that at the age of fourteen he was enabled, by God's grace, to give his heart to his God and Saviour; and at the same time he was admitted as a member of the class-meeting by the Rev. Mr. Pinkney.

He entered the English school connected with the chapel in Bangalore in 1856. He always manifested a love for learning. By his diligence and attention, under the Divine blessing, he made creditable progress, and obtained the approbation and goodwill of his teachers. After Mr. Pinkney left, he joined the class-meeting under the Rev. Mr. M'Cutchan. He used to express great gratitude for the advice and consolation he received at these meetings.

For several months previous to his decease his mind seemed to be much engaged on the subject of death, as appeared from the remarks he used to make in conversation, the purport of which may be expressed in the words of the Apostle, "For me to live is Christ, and to die is gain;" and still more from the feelings expressed in prayer; for he was accustomed to take a part in family devotions, and when it came to his turn to pray he invariably dwelt on the subject of death.

On the approach of death he betrayed nothing like fear. On the contrary, he rejoiced at the prospect of being "absent from the body and present with the Lord."

He died at Tripatore. The circumstances that led to his being there were these. Having a month's holiday in May, being the usual Midsummer vacation, he was anxious to avail himself of the same to enjoy a change, as well as to see his elder sister and her husband, who is employed as schoolmaster at Vaniembady, near Tripatore, as also to bring back his younger brother, who had been staying for some months with his sister.

He accordingly set out on the 9th of May, accompanied by his mother and two younger sisters. On the 11th they reached the village of Burgoor, near Tripatore, and, while staying here for the rest of the day, something remarkable occurred. He addressed his mother, and said, "Mother, when I retired for prayer, it seemed to me that I fell asleep and had a dream. A person approached me and said, 'After two days something will happen to you.' To which I replied, 'Lord forbid it.' He then said, 'But it will surely come.' On his saying so I awoke.

They reached Tripatore on the 12th. Almost immediately his sister Louisa, aged eleven years, was attacked by cholera. He said to her, "My dear sister, this ought to have come to me: why has it come to you?" By this illness they were prevented from prosecuting their journey. They remained in the house of the Catechist of the London Mission at Tripatore, who rendered all the aid in his power, and procured for her medical attendance. At nine o'clock that night there seemed to be a change for the better. Israel then read a portion of Scripture, and offered prayer. His brother-in-law was also present, having come in at seven o'clock in consequence of the intelligence of poor Louisa's illness.

On the 13th his sister and brother arrived from

Vaniembady. Then, too, he read the Bible and engaged in prayer. On the same day he wrote to his father, telling him how the Lord had been gracious to them in bringing them thus far, and requesting him to pray that God may bring them back in safety to see him once more. As usual, he conducted family worship that night.

In the morning of the following day (Saturday the 14th) his other younger sister, Charlotte, who was in her ninth year, was attacked by the same disease, and when he found that all the means made use of for her recovery seemed of no avail, he exhorted his mother and others not to exhibit sorrow in her presence, lest her faith should be shaken; and added, "Since she is about to leave this world of misery and go to the heavenly world of happiness, let us not sorrow for her, but let us sorrow on account of our sins, and then shall we have joy with her in heaven." The child died in the course of the day. To a question put to her by her mother a little before her death, as to what she was thinking about, she replied, "I am thinking of God, I am thinking of Jesus."

After the burial in the evening, Israel, weeping over the grave, said, "To-morrow I, too, shall sleep here." On returning to the house he read the 14th chapter of Job and the 90th Psalm, and engaged in prayer.

About midnight he was taken with cholera. When medicine was given him he took it willingly, but said at the same time, "I have no disease: the disease of my soul has been removed by the blood of my Saviour, and my soul is in health." On the morning of Sunday, the 15th, seeing his mother cry and the others sorrowing, he said, in a cheering tone, "Why are ye sorrowful? I shall not die." Shortly after this, evidently becoming worse, he prayed, saying, "O Lord, let me not suffer much, but take my soul soon to thyself." He then called for clean clothes, dressed himself, and, sitting up in bed, said, "The Lamb of God has taken my sister Charlotte to be his bride, and I am going to the marriage feast." To the question, "What do you say to me, my son?" asked by his mother, he replied, "Take care of my sister Louisa: go home soon to comfort my father. Be strong in faith." He then lay down, and, very soon after, asked for some water, which he drank, and, looking affectionately on those around him, he placed his right hand on his breast, and, pointing upwards, said in a low voice, "The Lord has opened the gate and is standing, the Lord has opened the gate and is standing;" and with these words on his lips his spirit took its flight from time into eternity at 11 A.M. of that Sabbath day. His body was committed to the grave in the evening, "In sure and certain hope of the resurrection to eternal life through our Lord Jesus Christ."

THANKS BE TO
GOD,
WHICH GIVETH US THE VICTORY
THROUGH OUR
LORD JESUS CHRIST.
1 COR. XV. 57.

THE HEART-MELTER.

THREE or four hundred Lutheran Hymns have been translated into the Tamil language for the benefit of the Tranquebar churches in India.

One day a Hindoo recited to an English Missionary, in the course of their conversation, the first verse of a beautiful hymn; when the latter, astonished, inquired of the stranger where he had found this verse. "Oh," replied he, "I have a book, 'the Heart-Melter,' which contains a great many such verses." As the Missionary had never heard of a book having this title, he wished to see it. The Hindoo produced it, wrapped up with great care, kissed it reverentially, and put it into the hands of the Missionary. And what was it? An old Tranquebar Hymn-book, to which, as the title page was lost, the Hindoo had given the name of "Heart-Melter," indicating thereby the heart-subduing influence it had excited upon himself.

"THY KINGDOM COME."

HAIL, Sun of righteousness! o'er heathen night
How blest the glories of Thy dawning light!
"Thy kingdom come!" What mean we by this prayer?
Already high in heaven, Thy throne is there.
"Thy kingdom come" *on earth;* O! let it spread
Where the deep waters cover ocean's bed;
Till all shall know Thee, all rejoice to own
The world Thine empire, and each heart Thy throne.

MISSIONARY NEWS.

I AM always glad to have news to tell you about the school children in foreign lands. You have already heard of Miss Ward's school of little black children in Belize. We have lately received a letter from Miss Ward, and she says—

"The children are very fond of Scripture history; sometimes I hear them talking after school about the Bible lesson which I have given in the morning. One evening I was amused to hear one of the girls comparing herself with David Some woman had threatened to beat her, as soon as she had an opportunity, and the girl was telling one of her companions about it. "But," said she, "I no 'fraid. You no 'member David and Goliath? Very well: dat same king, David, no 'fraid for de giant, and I no 'fraid for one big woman." They are all fond of school, especially the little ones. I wish you could see their bright little faces when they come into school, as though they think it the happiest place in the world.

One day I found one of them standing by the door after school had been dismissed, and when I asked her what she was waiting for, she said, in a very coaxing way, "Me no want go home, marm, me want tay wid you." She had only been at school a few days. One of the parents told me a few days ago that she cannot keep her children away from school, even when they are sick.

Some of the little girls work quite hard before they come to school in the morning, and begin work again as soon as they leave school. Even the little ones wash and iron very nicely.

CPSIA information can be obtained
at www.ICGtesting.com
Printed in the USA
LVHW040358200422
716646LV00005B/311

9 783752 593587